ONLY ONE LIFE

Jenny Mckean-Tinker

MINERVA PRESS
MONTREUX   LONDON   WASHINGTON

ONLY ONE LIFE
Copyright© Jenny Mckean-Tinker 1997

ISBN 1 86106 156 0

First published 1997 by
MINERVA PRESS
195 Knightsbridge
London SW7 1RE

Printed in Great Britain by
Antony Rowe Ltd, Chippenham, Wiltshire

ONLY ONE LIFE

This is for Sam, with all my love.
You jumped and I caught you.

About the Author

Brought up in Dorset, Jenny Mckean-Tinker has worked and travelled in Canada, Australia and Spain. She now lives and writes in Hampshire with her partner and two children. *Only One Life* is her first novel.

Chapter One

"Brilliant!" Lyddy braked as hard as she dared in the wet as an old dear in a Mini pulled out of a side turning. The Mini crawled along in front of her and she cursed under her breath, "Dear God! No second gear, either." The traffic lights coming up were green, but at this speed they were bound to change before she got there. They did and Lyddy's hands left the wheel, open palmed in exasperation. Why wasn't there an annual driving test for the over-seventies? At least it might remind them they've got an accelerator.

Lyddy glanced impatiently at the clock on the dash. She was nearly always late collecting the children. She thought of the reception she would probably get from Nikki. For a five year old, she was quite adept at turning situations to her advantage. She hated Lyddy being late and usually maintained her air of disapproval until a promise of some special treat was forthcoming. Lyddy had tried to explain that she couldn't help it and that she would always get there eventually. At least it was Friday, she could probably bring her round on the way home by discussing what they would do at the weekend. At seven, Peter was even tempered, not easily ruffled; he accepted having to wait with his usual good humour. But Lyddy felt guilty at keeping Peter's teacher hanging around again.

The rain was lashing down; the windscreen wipers were just coping. The lights changed and the old lady looked down for the gearstick. Lyddy turned the wheel hard to pull out round the back of the Mini and turn right. She managed to get across the path of the oncoming lorry and she accelerated away, wincing as she was treated to a flash of his lights and a blast from his horn. She was on the dual carriageway now and put her foot down.

Reaching over to push a cassette into the car stereo, she turned it on to distract her, and Tina Turner burst from the speakers. Lyddy turned the sound down a little. She moved into the outside lane and stayed there, checking the speedometer. She was doing ninety so she eased her foot off a little, in deference to the weather conditions.

Coming to the roundabout at the end, she started to relax, nearly there. A couple of turns and she was driving past the side of the school. There was no parking on the road outside the school railings; there had been a couple of accidents involving children coming out of school. By this time all the other children had gone home and Lyddy often pulled up onto the pavement to dash in and get Nikki and Peter. A policeman was standing in a doorway, just up the road, talking to the occupant of the house. "Oh, damn!" She decided to drive in through the school gates and park in the teachers' car park.

She switched off the engine, tucked her hair inside the neck of her coat and pulled up her collar. The rain was falling in torrents and she was soaked by the time she reached Peter's classroom. The door opened directly onto the playground; she threw it open and shut it quickly behind her. She shook the water from her hands and mussed her hair to lose some of its wetness.

"I'm sorry!" Lyddy directed this generally into the room.

Nikki and Peter were on the floor in one corner of the room, coats on, sticking coloured labels on the covers of a pile of books. Nikki's teacher took her up to wait with Peter when Lyddy was late.

Miss Carter, Peter's teacher, was kneeling on the floor in the middle of the room, sorting out folders of children's work. She looked up and smiled when Lyddy came into the room. She stood up with a pile of the folders in her arms, "Hi there." She was all in black: short skirt, baggy sweater, black tights. Her dark hair was cut short; she appeared quite young. Up closer, her face revealed one or two faint lines, evidence which her general appearance and enthusiasm belied. Thirties probably, thirty-four maybe.

Lyddy smiled back at her and moved across to the children. Peter looked up cheerfully, "Hi, Mum! Had a good day?"

She grinned; lovely boy. That was what she was supposed to ask him. "Yes, sweetheart. Have you?"

"Yup." He turned his face up to hers, lips pursed for a kiss.

Lyddy bent down to kiss him and ruffled his fair hair. "Sorry I'm late again. Have you been alright?"

"Oh, yes! Mrs Carlisle came in just now. She showed us the photographs from her skiing holiday." Mrs Carlisle was the headmistress. "There was one really funny one. She was stuck in a snowdrift. It didn't look like her - she had trousers on. It was funny, wasn't it, Nikki?"

Nikki looked up from the label she was peeling off. She didn't answer. The fair complexion of her cheeks was slightly flushed as it always was when she was annoyed about something. Lyddy stepped across and bent down to kiss her. Nikki didn't respond straight away, then she inclined her cheek reluctantly. But she wasn't going to offer a kiss in return.

Lyddy allowed herself a small smile. "Hello, darling. I'm sorry." She straightened up and walked over to where Miss Carter was slipping folders into drawers with children's names on them. "This is hopeless, isn't it? I always seem to get held up. I can't dash out of school the second the bell rings." Lyddy perched herself on the edge of a table as she spoke. "I had to see a parent today. She turned up in a bit of a stew just as I was leaving. I couldn't turn her away. You know what it's like."

Miss Carter knelt down again to get to the lower drawers and looked up, grinning at Lyddy's apologetic tone, "You needn't worry, really. It's no problem having them here. They've been helping me."

Lyddy went on, feeling some explanation was due. This wasn't the first time she had been late. "A friend of mine meets them three days a week. She can't manage the other two days now - she's started work herself. I'm going to have to find someone else to do it."

Miss Carter sat back on her heels as she listened. Lyddy ran her hand through her wet hair in her frustration at the situation. "We finish at three and I try to get away by twenty past if I'm collecting the children." She glanced out of the window, "It's a fifteen minute drive on a good day, but on a day like today all the crazies seem to get their cars out." Her eyes rolled upwards in their sockets. "It was the zimmer frame brigade today."

Miss Carter laughed. "Where do you teach?"

Lyddy told her the name of the school and Miss Carter's face registered surprise, "I live a couple of roads up from there. Hawthorn Lane."

"Do you really? Is that the road with the row of white cottages in?" Lyddy asked.

"Mm. I live in the end one, next to the woods."

"What a lovely place to live."

Miss Carter's expression acknowledged that she thought so too. Then her eyebrows went up, "You do that in fifteen minutes?"

Lyddy laughed. "On a good day. I haven't had a ticket yet."

Miss Carter slipped the last folder away and reached for her coat lying across a table. She stood holding it in her arms, looking at Lyddy, "Which days does your friend meet the children?"

"Tuesdays, Wednesdays and Thursdays," Lyddy answered, wondering what was in her mind.

She was obviously thinking through an idea. She made her decision. "I could take them home with me on Mondays and Fridays. I'm always here till late on the other days but I get in really early on a Monday. I can be away by about ten to four, unless we have a meeting." She smiled, "I'm usually ready for home, anyway." She went on, "And on Fridays I try to escape as well. I take work home with me and do it at the weekend."

Lyddy looked apologetic, glancing at her watch. "Oh, yes. You've made a really fast getaway today, haven't you?"

Miss Carter grinned at her. "It doesn't matter. I don't just run straight out of the door. There's always something to do."

Lyddy's brow creased slightly as she considered the suggestion. It seemed an imposition. "I couldn't ask you to do that, it would be too much."

"You haven't asked me. I've offered. At least I could do it until you get something else sorted out. I can't see that it would put me out much." She paused, then added, "You would have to drop a note into the office." All arrangements concerning collection of children had to be held in writing by the school. A sign of the times.

Nikki appeared at Lyddy's side, tugging on her sleeve, "Mum, when are we going?"

"Wait a minute, sweetheart. I'm just coming." Lyddy took her hand.

"Mum, I'm hungry. I want to go home." She pulled Lyddy's hand.

"Wait a minute!" Lyddy looked at her, a severe look which told her not to interrupt. Peter was standing at the door, opening and closing it to feel the blast of weather which came in each time.

"Peter! Don't do that, please." She turned back to Miss Carter who was standing, waiting patiently, an amused expression around her eyes.

"Look. Why don't you think about it," Lyddy said. "It's a marvellous offer but I'd hate to think that you might have made it on impulse and then regretted it later."

"No," Miss Carter shook her head and smiled. "Just say yes. Make life more manageable." Then she added, good-humouredly, "I might as well be on my way home with them as waiting here."

Lyddy returned a rueful smile, "It would be great." She was relenting, thinking that it would help her out, do away with that hectic dash on Mondays and Fridays. It would give her more time in school after her last class. Miss Carter sensed her giving in. "Okay, then. We'll start on Monday, shall we?"

"Terrific," Lyddy was grateful. "I'll give you my home number and I'd better give you the school number as well just in case there's a problem any day. You could get a message to me if you needed to." She felt in her coat pocket and pulled out an old envelope and bent down to write the phone numbers on it. She passed the envelope to Miss Carter.

"Mu-um!" Nikki was getting fed up, tugging again.

"Alright, sweetheart. We're going now."

"I live in the end house, number fourteen," Miss Carter said. "I'll see you on Monday. Say about four-fifteen." She walked with Lyddy and Nikki to the door where Peter stood with his foot holding it ajar, letting the wind blow his hair through the gap.

"I'm really grateful," said Lyddy. "I'll make other arrangements as soon as I can. But let me know if it doesn't work out for you."

"Fine." It was dismissed as unlikely. "Come on you two." Miss Carter bundled Nikki and Peter out of the door. "You'll have to run or you'll get drenched." She pulled her coat over her head and made a dash across the playground towards the office, turning as she ran, "Have a good weekend!"

They ran to the car and piled in out of the rain. Lyddy waited while they buckled themselves in.

"What were you talking about, Mum?" asked Peter as Lyddy started the engine.

"I'll tell you later, darling. I want to think about it first. Let's get home; I'm starving." She backed out of the parking space and drove out through the school gates, glancing bleakly up at the low, dark clouds emptying down on them, hoping this wasn't going to last all weekend. February was usually a cold month. She couldn't remember it being so wet before at this time of year. Oh, roll on spring.

She turned into the driveway ten minutes later. The house was a red-bricked semi-detached, built in the late thirties, the gravelled drive taking up most of the front garden. It meant she could turn the car round in the drive instead of having to back it out onto the road. There was no garage but a wide, gravelled path leading to the gate at the back of the house.

The rain had eased slightly for a while. They all got out of the car, the children pushing in at the front door waiting for Lyddy to unlock it. She opened the door and switched on the hall light. It was nearly dark inside the house, the late afternoon was so dull.

"Dodger!" Nikki bent down to put her arms around the shaggy dog. He was part Labrador, part Border Collie and other parts as well. His tail was wagging furiously as usual, delighted to see them all home. Lyddy let him have the run of the house while they were out.

"Did Mr Burpy take you for a nice walk today, Dodge?" Nikki had recovered her good humour. She rolled on the floor, hugging Dodger and taking him over with her.

"If Mr Burberry finds out you still call him that, you'll be for it," Lyddy told her. Mr Burberry was an ex-neighbour, in his seventies. He walked Dodger in the morning and took him home with him and then walked him back in the afternoon. He had a key to the house. As a toddler, learning to talk, Nikki had called him Mr Burpy and the name had stuck. "And go and get changed before you start rolling around," Lyddy added. Peter had already gone upstairs to get out of his uniform.

Lyddy went through to the kitchen at the back of the house, turning the heating on, switching on lights and hanging her coat up. She glanced through the open doors as she passed, everything was always clean and tidy on a Friday; Mrs Page did a thorough job. Lyddy hated housework. It was worth working full-time to have it done for her.

She loved this house, the children did too. It was their haven. She was always pleased to arrive home, especially on a Friday night. She started the routine in the kitchen, Dodger padding round after her, reminding her that he was to be fed as well. It was a large kitchen with an old pine table in the middle. It reminded Lyddy of a farmhouse kitchen and they spent a lot of time in it. She had a dining room but the three of them ate their meals in the kitchen. It was warm and comfortable. The children did their paintings, drawings, puzzles and such at the table while Lyddy was occupied in there.

They had been in the house for about six months and Lyddy still felt delighted by it; the novelty hadn't worn off. After David's death she had wanted a home of her own, not a reminder of the past. The other house had held too many memories, not all pleasant. She often reflected on how their lives had changed for the better when they moved.

She put Dodger's dinner down for him and searched the cassette rack on the wall. She chose Kirsty MacColl and slipped it into the cassette player on the shelf.

As she prepared the meal, she thought about the arrangement with Peter's teacher, looking for snags. It seemed a bit daft, the children having to trek nearly over to where she worked and then having to get back in the car to be driven home again. But Lyddy had to pass the end of her road on the way from work to the children's school as they lived on the edge of the catchment area. It wasn't actually that far back from Miss Carter's to their house. And it was only two days a week. She decided that she would leave the arrangement as it was; it helped her out for the moment.

The phone rang and she picked it up.

"Lyddy, it's Jane."

Lyddy gave a short laugh, "You want to know what I'm wearing tonight?"

"What? No, I don't! Bloody party. What are you wearing, anyway?"

"I don't know yet. Can I go casual?"

"Well, knowing Tom and Margaret, you could probably go in your birthday suit and they wouldn't notice."

"Oh, good, that solves a problem. Who's driving?"

"Me. Listen. My brother has two tickets for Victoria Wood. He can't use them. Interested?"

"When is it?" Lyddy asked. Jane told her. Lyddy grabbed the saucepan lid off the potatoes just as they threatened to boil over and turned the gas down a bit. "Wonderful," she said. "What about Jack? Doesn't he want to go?"

"You're joking. He walks out when she's on the box. Says she's a woman's comedian. Just an excuse to go to the pub, I think."

"Right. I'll put it on the calendar."

"Great. I must get cracking with dinner. We'll pick you up at eight."

"Okay. See you later." Lyddy put the phone down and heard Peter and Nikki coming down the stairs, arguing. They jostled each other coming into the kitchen, each trying to get to her first to give their side of the story.

"Mum! Peter's torn my batman cloak. Look! He did it on purpose."

"Mum, it was an accident. I fell off the bed."

"You shouldn't have been playing with it! It's not yours!"

"Well, you play with my things."

They both spoke at once, both gabbling on, one accusing, one defending. In the end she put her hands up. "For goodness sake! Let me see."

Nikki ignored her, carrying on her tirade.

"Nikki, stop! Let me look at it. I can mend it, look here. I've got that black sticky tape."

Nikki opened her mouth to protest again.

"Nikki, enough! It was an accident. It'll mend."

Nikki subsided, "Well, he should have asked me if he could play with it, Mum." She pouted, flushed as usual when put out. She looked crossly at Peter, "Bum face!" Her name-calling had become noticeably more imaginative since she had started school in September.

Lyddy controlled the urge to grin. "Nikki! Don't say that."

"Well, he is." She turned back to Peter. "You pumpous old wind bag!" she darted at him.

Peter laughed; it was guaranteed to incite her further. "Pumpous!" He tossed his head back, exaggerating his scorn, "It's not pumpous, stupid. It's pompous!"

Lyddy held Nikki by the shoulder before she felt obliged to retaliate in a more demonstrative way. "Okay. No more. Peter, go and wash your hands. You too, Nikki. Tea's nearly ready. Let's be quick; I'm going out tonight."

Nikki was distracted from defending her honour, "Who's baby-sitting, Mum?"

"Annie, sweetheart."

"Are we going to stay at her house?"

"No, she's coming here."

"Oh! Why can't we...?"

Lyddy interrupted her, "Because it's all arranged. Now, go and wash your hands. Go!"

They went through to the washroom leading off from the small utility room and she heard them laughing as they pushed each other to get to the sink first. Lyddy started putting food on the plates, happy that it was the weekend. She sang out, joining in the song coming from the stereo,

"Don't come the cowboy with me, Sonny Jim."

"Mu-um!" The chorus came from the washroom.

She grinned and sang out louder,

"I've known lots of those,

And you're not one of them."

Nikki appeared at the doorway, holding the hand towel with outstretched arms above her head. She swayed her body and rolled her eyes upwards, exaggerating her crooning style as she sang.

"Oh-oh, de-ar," she rested on the note for a moment before she sang on,

"Mother's got the singin' bloo-oos."

Peter appeared behind her, making a face at the racket, "Women!"

Lyddy's eyes widened and she laughed, "Peter!"

Chapter Two

A month later, half term had come and gone. They had been back at school for a week, back in the chaotic routine of the morning rush.

Lyddy glanced at the clock on the wall, nearly eight o'clock. She could never understand how the time went so quickly first thing in the morning. Nikki had finished her breakfast and was on the floor wrestling with a doll and its dress. Peter was at the table tying a piece of string to a toy ladder, his toast forgotten on his plate.

"Nikki, go upstairs and get your shoes. Go to the toilet before we go. Peter, leave that. Finish your toast. Peter! Leave it!" She reached across and took the toy from him, putting it up on a shelf. "Eat your toast. Hurry up!"

She started to clear the rest of the table, putting dirty cups and plates in the sink, emptying leftovers into the bin. The phone rang. "Oh, bloody hell!" she muttered under her breath. Why were Monday mornings always like this? "Hello?" She held the phone with one hand while she wiped crumbs off the table.

"Lyddy? It's Annie."

Her sister, she should know better than to ring at this hour. Lyddy tried not to show her impatience. "Annie. You'll have to be quick. I'm running really late."

She directed her voice away from the phone for a moment, "Peter, go and put your coat on and find your reader. It's got to go back today. Hurry!" She turned her attention back to the phone, "Annie, sorry." She paused to let Annie get to the point.

"Lyddy, I'm sorry. I'll be really quick. You couldn't give me a lift to the garage to pick up the car after school, could you? I've got to take it in this morning; it's going to be in all day. I'll have to miss my keep-fit class."

"Okay. I'll come round after I've got the children, about half four." Lyddy would rather have suggested that Annie got a cab but couldn't bring herself to. She owed Annie more favours than she cared to remember.

"You're sure you don't mind? It won't put you out?" Typical Annie, ask a favour and then prepare to spend five minutes apologising.

"No, Annie. That's fine. I must go. I'm going to be late. I'll see you later." She put the phone down, glancing bleakly at the washing up. Mrs Page would do it but Lyddy knew she disapproved of a mother who couldn't even leave the kitchen tidy in the morning.

Five minutes later, they were in the car. Lyddy pulled out of the drive going through her mental check list of things she might have forgotten.

"Mum! I haven't got my reader!"

"Oh, Peter. I reminded you! I haven't got time to go back now. You'll have to take it tomorrow."

She listened to his wailing but didn't answer. She turned right and pulled into the drive of a detached house, double garage, newly-built brick wall fronting the garden. Jane appeared at the front door drying her hands on a towel. Lyddy waved to her through the windscreen. "Out you get, quickly. Nikki, don't forget your snack box. Give me a kiss."

The children leant over the front seats to kiss her and got out of the car. Peter closed the door behind him and Lyddy let the front passenger window down to speak to him. "Peter, remember, you go with Miss Carter after school today. I'll see you there." She raised her voice, "Bye, Nikki!"

"Bye, Mum!" Nikki was disappearing through the front door. They had some time to spend with Jane's children before leaving for school.

Peter stood with his face at the open window. "Bye Mum. See you later. I love you."

"Love you, sweetheart. Have a nice day."

Peter followed Nikki into the house. Lyddy put the car into reverse as Jane called out, "Have a good weekend?"

"Yes, thanks. Must dash. I'll see you tomorrow." She mustn't get drawn into conversation with Jane. She'd never get away. Jane took the cue and waved, going back into the house.

Lyddy relaxed as she drove off. She liked to be in school half an hour before the bell. Getting out of the house was a daily battle she thought she would never get used to and she wondered how many years the stress of the effort was costing her. She looked at the clock; she was okay for time even allowing for Monday morning traffic.

She had started working full-time in September when Nikki started school. She had already been part-time, teaching drama in the lower school and then became full-time when they needed someone to take some more GCSE English classes. She liked the drama better but had been lucky to land herself full-time work so easily after a break in teaching. She was finding it hard work fitting everything in, especially with all the record keeping and the planning involved now, but she enjoyed her independence these days. For that alone, it was worth all the effort.

She mulled over the weekend as she drove. The weather had been wonderful - crisp sunshine in the morning and warm enough to go without coats in the afternoon. The gardens were beginning to show some colour. The camellias were already blooming and some early rhododendrons were out. The flowering cherry in her garden was about to burst into blossom.

She had taken the children down to Lulworth Cove on Saturday. They walked Dodger up along the cliff top and then had lunch outside a pub. They spent the afternoon climbing over rocks on a crab hunt, walking the pebbly, sweeping beach, collecting shells and washed up debris. Not a cloud in the sky, it had been glorious.

She thought how much more she enjoyed weekends now that she was working full-time. It was the reward at the end of a hard week. She made a deliberate effort to do only essential jobs around the house on Saturdays and Sundays, and to do something special with the children on at least one of the days.

Lyddy still marvelled at how life was turning out and felt good about it. Only a little more than a year ago, she had felt dreary, life had been dreary. She still shuddered inwardly at the thought. That other person she had been then was a stranger to her now. Living with David had been a constant battle to maintain some sense of importance in herself, a battle she had perpetually lost. At thirty-six, she had felt like the little wife, whose life was confined to that role with no other contribution to make. David had scoffed at her when she tried to talk to him about it. She had seen how quietly and subtly he ruled and directed their lives, but she had seemed unable to rise out of the rut. She'd won one battle when she accepted the part-time teaching job without consulting him first, much to his chagrin and long-lasting displeasure. But even that hadn't made much real difference. That was when it had really sunk in that life with David was always going to be like that.

She brought her thoughts back to the here and now, pushing away her guilt which came with the relief of no longer having to cope with such apparently insoluble problems. She turned into the driveway of the school. Some of the early kids were dawdling up the pathway, green uniforms, rucksacks and school bags slung over their shoulders, exchanging news of their weekend, the younger ones larking about on the way.

She found a parking space and collected up her piles of marking and her bag, locked the car door and headed off towards the staffroom to check the noticeboard and her pigeon-hole.

By quarter past four that afternoon, Lyddy was turning into Hawthorn Lane. She'd had a good day but always felt tired after the first day of the week. She had lost her free periods to cover for someone else so she'd brought home another pile of marking to do. She'd had to write a report after school over an incident with two girls. Lyddy had turned the corner in the corridor to see one of them punch the other on the nose. The victim had had to go to hospital, her nose broken. The assailant was very bright but a rough piece of work; this would see her suspended. Lyddy quite liked the girl, but she'd gone too far this time.

She parked the car in front of the last house in the row. She loved these cottages, white-washed, with slate roofs and small windows denoting their age. The end of the terrace, number fourteen, had a driveway at the side leading to a garage at the back. The stick-like trails of a clematis were trained over much of the front of the house, the leaf buds just visible. It would be covered in flowers in a month or two.

Miss Carter's car was parked just inside the driveway. Lyddy was pleased at the way the arrangement was working out. She was good company for the children, her sense of humour rarely wearing off, even at the end of a tiring day with a class of thirty. Nikki and Peter enjoyed going with her and were always full of it on their way home. Lyddy had worried that Nikki might protest but she had warmed to Miss Carter's sense of fun. Lyddy felt at ease now, able to relax; the arrangement was plainly not felt to be a burden. She usually stayed for a cup of tea before going home and they were getting to know each other. It had lifted them out of the formal parent-teacher relationship. Lyddy liked her.

She raised the heavy knocker on the front door and let it go gently. Miss Carter opened the door almost at once. She had changed out of her working clothes and wore a loose shirt tucked into jeans; they showed off her slim waist. She looked younger and taller, slightly taller than Lyddy, probably five eight.

"Hi! Come in. The children are out in the garden. I'm guinea pig sitting for two weeks. My neighbours have gone on holiday."

Lyddy smiled, "I'll have a job tearing Nikki away. She's desperate to have a rabbit. I won't get any peace until I say yes." She stepped through the doorway and held up a bottle of gin.

"Is that for now? I was going to offer you a cup of tea but I've got some tonic."

Lyddy grinned. "No, it's for you. I thought it was time to say thank you for having the children for me. I took a flier on what you'd like. Do you drink gin?"

"I drink anything." She led the way through the sitting room.

It was a long room which stretched to the back of the house, the rear of it serving as a dining area with an old oak table and chairs. French windows looked out onto the back garden. A large open hearth graced the sitting room area, the sofa and easy chairs pushed up to surround it. The ash remains of a fire lay in the grate.

They went into the kitchen and Miss Carter looked at Lyddy as she took cups out of the cupboard. "It's not necessary, you know. The bottle, I mean. I never refuse booze but you needn't have bothered."

"Well, I didn't think you would take money so this is what I decided on."

"Thank you. I accept with grace." She took the bottle and put it on the fridge. "Will you have a cup of tea before you go?"

"Yes, thanks. I mustn't be long. I've got to take my sister to the garage to pick up her car." Lyddy looked out of the kitchen window. "I'll just say hello to the children." She stepped out of the back door. Nikki and Peter were crouched down on the grass, feeding daisies to the guinea pig.

"Hi, sweethearts." They both looked up, faces radiant. She would have to give in over the rabbit but decided on a pep-talk first. They would have to look after it, clean its hutch, feed it and water it.

"Hi, Mum." Nikki smiled at her. "Look. This is Gertrude."

"She's lovely, isn't she?" Lyddy bent down to kiss them both and stroke the guinea pig.

"Well, she's a he, actually," said Peter. "They thought he was a girl when he was little so they called him Gertrude, but the vet said he's a boy. I think they should have changed his name, don't you, Mum?"

Lyddy smiled her agreement and straightened up. She started back towards the house, calling behind her as she went, "I'm just going to have a quick cup of tea. Don't be long. We're taking up Miss Carter's time."

"Call me Chris." She was standing in the open doorway watching them. "I hate being called 'Miss' out of school. It makes me feel like an old spinster."

"Spinster," Lyddy laughed at the word. She stopped at the doorway. "Well, you must call me Lydia, Lyddy actually. I hate the name Lydia."

"Lyddy, okay. And you're not holding me up. Have your tea. Come and sit down." Chris carried the cups through to the dining table. "Have you had a good day?" She sat down at one end of the table.

Lyddy followed her and sat on a chair facing the French windows. She stretched her legs out in front of her and sat back with her hands behind her head. "Tiring. I find Mondays a bit hard going, getting back into it after the weekend."

"I know what you mean. I had to go up to Manchester yesterday. I didn't get back till eleven o'clock last night. I'm shattered today." She looked at Lyddy as she went on, "My ex-boyfriend's mum had a fall last week." She grimaced and raised her eyebrows. "Somehow I got roped in to going up there to bring her down to stay with him while she recovers. I'm not sure why I got the job, but never mind." She glanced out of the window and looked back at Lyddy, amusement in her eyes. "It was a bit of a cheek, really, seeing as we split up in October. He phoned me out of the blue; he's lost his licence, apparently. Anyway, I was so taken aback I didn't think to say no." She laughed at herself, having been taken in.

"How long did you go out with him?" Lyddy leant forward to pick up her cup. She enjoyed the opportunity to relax for five minutes before heading for home. Annie would have to wait.

"Well, we went out for about eighteen months. Then he moved in with me and we lived together for three years. But in the end the house wasn't big enough for the two of us," she grinned, "metaphorically speaking."

She was one of those people who can find the funny side of life. Lyddy liked her for it. It was probably why she was so good with the kids at school.

"You didn't part amicably, I take it?"

Chris laughed before she answered, "I suppose you could say that. Which is why it was such a cheek to phone me about his mum." Her amusement still showed in her face, "Actually, I left him drunk in a bar in Seville."

Lyddy raised her eyebrows, waiting for Chris to tell her story.

"We'd taken an apartment in Portugal for a week at half term. I can't remember the name of the place. One day we hired a car and drove over the border to Seville. It's about a hundred miles or something. Anyway, after sightseeing and wandering around, we sat outside a bar after lunch. You know how everything stops in the afternoon over there. Bill got really drunk on red wine. He started accusing me of not needing him and not showing enough interest in him, his work, et cetera."

She shook her head, indicating that the details weren't important. "I was watching him, you know, studying him. It was like looking at him for the first time. And I suddenly thought, it's true, I don't need him. I'd really been keeping out of his way as much as I could. Do you know how those situations creep up on you and suddenly hit you in the face?" She looked at Lyddy to see if she understood.

Lyddy gave a wry smile, thinking back over the last years with David. "Don't I just," she said.

Chris went on, "Well, I suddenly realised that I was bored with him. I *had* lost interest in him. Anyway," she decided to cut out the finer points, "on the spur of the moment, I told him I was going home, and I did! I just couldn't face the rest of the holiday with him."

Lyddy said dryly, "You're obviously an impetuous person."

Chris considered this. "Yes, I suppose I am. I always seem to decide the important things on impulse."

She carried on with her story. It wasn't finished yet. "Anyway, Bill positively spluttered. He was very drunk. I hitched back to Portugal; got a lift with an American couple going to Faro. They took me back to the apartment and waited while I collected my things and then took me to Faro airport." She was smiling at her obvious triumph over her luck and her audacity.

"I got the first flight home I could get, packed up his stuff and took it round to his old flat. His flatmate still lives there. Well, he lives there too now,"

"Did he come rushing back after you?"

"You're joking. He stayed to the end of the week. He wouldn't waste the money we'd paid for the apartment!" Chris laughed. "In fact, when he got back, he came round here and I wasn't sure which he was most annoyed about: me dumping him in the middle of the holiday or him having to pay an extra day on the rented car because he'd been too drunk to drive it back to Portugal that day."

Lyddy grinned, but she was envious of the simplicity of it all. "It's so much easier when there are no children, isn't it?" She leant forward to put her empty cup on the table.

Chris's smile faded as she looked at Lyddy. She knew of her husband's death early last year. "Did you have a tough time?" she asked.

"Well, yes. I suppose I did." Lyddy looked at her watch and relaxed her features to lighten the mood. She didn't want to get into all that now, anyway she had sat for too long. "It's all in the past now," she glanced at Chris and smiled. "All the wounds are just about healed." She stood up, wishing she could stay for longer. "And I've got to go. My sister's not going to be very impressed with me."

She walked to the kitchen door, still open onto the garden. It was getting chilly now. Nikki and Peter were sorting through an unlit bonfire at the bottom of the garden. The guinea pig sat on top of its hutch. She called out through the doorway, "Nikki! Peter! Put Gertrude back in his hutch. We must go. Come on! We've got to go and collect Annie."

She stepped back into the kitchen, "Thanks for the tea, Chris. Now for the evening rush. You know, tea, baths, stories, bed." She made a face, "I've got piles of marking to do tonight, as well."

Chris had followed her into the kitchen and was leaning against a cupboard. She sympathised, "I wonder at the stamina of working mums. Do you find it hard?"

"Sometimes. You have to be organised, which I'm not, and you have to have a mental list of priorities." Lyddy grinned, "Things like ironing get stuck somewhere at the bottom of it. Not that that bothers me much. I must say, I look forward to the weekends."

Chris had been standing watching her. "Why don't you all stay and have tea here sometime. What about Friday? You can relax more on a Friday, can't you? No school the next day."

Lyddy thought. "What, this Friday? Okay. That would be nice." She added with a smile, "I won't have to cook for once." She looked back at the children putting Gertrude in his hutch, giving him a daisy through the wire mesh. "I'm sure they'll be delighted."

She called out again into the garden, "Come on, you two." They didn't react. "I'm going! Bye!"

"Mum! Wait!"

Nikki and Peter came tumbling into the kitchen. They relaxed when they saw her waiting.

"Peter!" Lyddy exclaimed when she saw him. "Look at your trousers!" They were daubed with mud and bits of debris from the bonfire.

"Oh, look at your shoes!" This was directed at both of them; the soles of their shoes were caked in thick, wet mud.

Nikki looked down in surprise, "Oh, my gawd!"

"Nikki! For goodness sake, don't say that." Lyddy pressed her lips together to keep a straight face and glanced at Chris, daring her to laugh. She pushed the two of them back out into the garden. "Don't come in here. Go round the side, I'll meet you at the front."

She walked though the house, Chris went with her. "Go on, say it: 'The things they pick up at school.' Don't blame us. I can't remember seeing the use of 'Oh, my gawd' in the National Curriculum."

Lyddy laughed with her. "That's nothing. You should hear her when she's cross. Her use of language has taken a colourful turn recently."

She opened the front door and stepped outside. Chris leant in the doorway, hands shoved in the pockets of her jeans. "See you on Friday. Hope you get all your marking done."

Lyddy smiled. "There's always tomorrow." She raised a hand in farewell and walked towards the car where Nikki and Peter were waiting, discussing something animatedly. Chris stood watching them, their voices drifting across the front garden to where she was standing.

"Mum? When *can* I have a rabbit?"

"It wouldn't just be your rabbit."

"Yes, it would. Boys don't have rabbits."

"Of course they do, stupid."

"Peter, don't call her stupid." Lyddy unlocked the car.

"Mum? When can I have a rabbit?"

"Get in. We'll talk about it in the car. Strap yourselves in. Get your muddy shoes off the seats!"

She waved to Chris as she drove off and saw her go back into the house.

Chapter Three

A few days later, Lyddy sat at her desk in the sitting room, the lamp beside her the only lighting in the room. She picked up the pile of books in front of her and leant over to dump them on the sofa. She pulled the last pile across the desk towards her and sat back in her chair, relaxing for a moment. She wondered when to do the food shop in Sainsbury's. She couldn't do it after school tomorrow as they were staying for tea at Chris Carter's and she hated dragging the children round on a Saturday morning. She decided she would dash out at lunch time tomorrow. She must remember to leave Mr Burberry his money for the morning and a note to ask him to keep Dodger for the afternoon.

Lyddy became aware that the stereo was silent and got up to put another CD on. She knelt down to choose one, deciding she would get herself a glass of wine to keep her going at the marking. She smiled inwardly, thinking of how her drinking habits had changed over the last year. She'd virtually stopped drinking during the last few years of her marriage. Associating drinking with relaxing, she'd just lost the taste for it. She thought how uptight she had been most of the time and cringed. Good God! What a way to have lived. She often had a glass now, even at home on her own, and frequently over-indulged in company. Her only scruple was the threat of dealing with a hangover the next day.

She chose some music and pressed the start button on the CD player. Dodger got up and followed her into the kitchen, looking up at her hopefully. "No Dodger, you greedy mutt. No food." She bent down to rub her hand over his shaggy head and walked to the fridge to take out an opened bottle. The door bell rang and she glanced at her watch, wondering who might be calling at this hour. It was nearly ten o'clock.

She unlocked the front door and opened it, holding Dodger's collar with her spare hand. He was growling softly, punctuating the growl with short, low barks.

"Hello, my darling. Am I disturbing you?"

Lyddy's face echoed her delight. "Will! What are you doing here?"

He wore a broad smile. "Come to see if you're still alive. Is it too late to come in?" He held out a bottle of Jacob's Creek.

"Of course not," Lyddy met him as he stepped over the door sill and hugged him tightly. She pushed the front door shut and shushed Dodger who was giving excited little barks, jostling around Will's feet. She put her arm through Will's as they walked through to the kitchen. "Come and take your coat off. I've been marking; I was just going to have a drink. How are you?" She hugged his arm as she spoke.

"I'm fine. A bit worn out." Will was a solicitor and put in incredibly long hours, the price of success. He was very ambitious.

Lyddy took the bottle from him. "I won't open this. I've got one in the fridge."

Will took off his coat and lay it on the kitchen table. He leant against the back of a chair with his arms crossed, watching as Lyddy poured the drinks. He was very dark featured, almost olive skinned, his black hair curly, and he always looked in need of a shave by the end of the day.

"How have you been?" he said, still smiling at her.

Lyddy passed him the bottle to take with them and hugged him again before she picked up the two glasses. "All the better for seeing you. Let's go into the sitting room."

She threw her piles of books onto an armchair and they sat one each end of the sofa, she with her legs curled under her and he with his stretched out in front of him, half turned towards her. They chinked glasses.

He glanced at her desk, "Am I holding you up?"

"No, you're the excuse I needed. I'm on the last pile. They're not desperate – I'll do them at the weekend."

"Well, I won't stay long." Will looked at her, pleased he had decided to drop in. "You're starting to look smugly content with life. Have you found a lover I don't know about?"

Lyddy's eyes laughed; he often inquired on this score. "No! I've told you, I think I'm done with all that." Then she said, "I wouldn't know what to do with a lover any more."

Will didn't agree. "It would come back." He grinned at her. "Do you fancy coming round for a meal on Saturday? Nothing elaborate. We just decided we haven't been very hospitable lately – working too hard, I suppose." He went through a list of people who were also invited.

"Will, I would have loved to, but I've just invited my dad for the weekend." She had phoned her father earlier that evening. She made a face to show her disappointment. "It's three years this Sunday that Mum died. He still gets a bit morose if he's on his own. Annie or I always have him to stay; the children cheer him up." She looked apologetically at Will. "He would baby-sit for me, but I couldn't leave him on his own, not this weekend."

Will understood and he put his hands up to show that further explanations were unnecessary. "A pity. I had someone lined up for you." His face creased in a grin again, "Forty, separated, good looking. A new chap at work. I told him about you. I told him you would feel a gooseberry without a partner." He watched Lyddy, awaiting her reaction.

"You didn't! Did he think you were serious?"

"Yes, of course. He probably wouldn't have accepted otherwise," he replied dryly.

Lyddy raised her eyebrows and tutted at Will's nerve. "How *is* Carl, by the way? Working too hard, I suppose?"

Will shrugged and lifted his hands in resignation. "He's doing so well, that's the trouble. He's just been up to London for three days. He got back yesterday." Carl ran his own business, selling cars, mostly at the upper end of the market.

"You two are workaholics."

"Well, he's talking about getting a manager in. He really doesn't need to do all the slog now." Will shrugged again, thinking of his own workload, "We've got this new guy at work. After this case he will take over some of my work."

Lyddy looked at Will with fond concern, "Well, that sounds hopeful. You two must hardly see each other."

Will and Carl had been together for about eight years, having met just before she and David married. Before that, Lyddy had seen a succession of boyfriends come and go. She liked Carl; he was such fun. She remembered back to the days when she, David, Will and Carl had sometimes made up a foursome. David had only gone because she said she would go without him if he didn't. It was one of the few occasions that she had put her foot down with him. David hadn't been jealous of her close friendship with Will, but resentful. Why did she still need Will after she was married? He also incessantly made reference to Will and Carl's relationship. He never felt comfortable around them. Carl picked up on David's feelings, but didn't care; in fact he played on them. He would take Will's hand over the table in a restaurant or peck him on the cheek in a bar, things which he would never normally have done. They didn't ram their relationship down other people's throats. David would look very embarrassed and excuse himself to go to the toilet and they would all roar with laughter when he was out of earshot.

Lyddy topped up her glass and poured the last dregs into Will's; he was driving. They talked on, exchanging gossip and news.

Lyddy always felt happy in Will's company. They had known each other for years; they met when she was a student and he in his first solicitor's job. They used to frequent the same pub and somehow their two groups had all gone to a party together. She had got very drunk sitting at the top of the stairs of the house, sharing a bottle of whisky with Will. Oddly enough, there had never been any romantic notions on her part. They had become friends and had known each other for about three months before Will told her he was gay. It seemed incredible now that she hadn't picked up any cue when they were out in a group, but then she hadn't been looking. She and Will became very close. They laughed a lot, mostly at themselves; argued a lot, passionate debates; and drank a lot, mocking the world at large. But she soon realised that he was very caring underneath all the banter. He had more than the average share of empathy with other people, particularly with those close to him. She'd had fun with Will, but also he soon became the one she went to with her problems. He was the one she confided in, the bad and the good. She had cried on his shoulder more than once.

Will had been telling her about the case he was working on. He was one of the senior partners now and getting all the big stuff. He revelled in it. He changed the subject, putting work aside, studying her in the low light, his expression showing his fondness for her.

"You're really happy here, aren't you?" He looked around the room, "In this house, I mean. On your own. You're blooming, you know."

"Thank you, my darling. That's the nicest comment I've had today." Lyddy uncoiled her legs and stretched them out in front of her so that she wouldn't get pins and needles. She pulled her sweatshirt down over her jeans and lay back holding her glass on her chest and looked a little smug. She thought for a moment. "I'm very content these days." Her look apologised for being a bit corny. She glanced around her, wondering just where this feeling of self-satisfaction had its origin then she looked back to Will. "I like being my own boss," she declared, almost defiantly. "I like controlling my own life."

The corner of Will's mouth turned up, "Yes, I can see that."

"Are you laughing at me?"

Will put his hands up with a grin, "I wouldn't dare."

"You would dare. And you are!"

"I'm not." He wiped the merriment off his expression with an effort, "Do I see an ardent feminist emerging from its cocoon?"

She sat up. "Oh, rubbish, Will!" Then she checked herself, "Why is it that word always sounds derogatory? Why do I always sense an accusation?"

He kept his smile off his face, "Not in my case. And you are a feminist." He paused, about to make his point, "Are you or are you not revelling in your emancipation, your throwing off of the chains?"

"I'm enjoying living off my own wits, that's all. It doesn't have to be labelled."

"Have you or have you not declared yourself unneedful of a male?"

She turned towards him, indignant, "That's not feminism! I simply meant I'm happy as I am. There you are, that's my point! Being a feminist doesn't at all mean doing without men. I just happen not to want one. And you're not in court now, you know," she said. Then her bottom jaw set as something snapped and she went on the attack, raising her voice in her exasperation, "What is this? Why can't I be happy on my own? Why do people seem to think that I have to have a mate or cease to exist? The world won't stop turning just because I happen to be thinking, breathing, providing for myself." She caught the trace of a smile around Will's eyes and it incited her further. "Just because I'm not fitting the mould cast for me, why do I have to be labelled? Maybe I am a feminist but in the true sense of the word, and it needn't be assumed that that is my guiding light. I am who I am. I'm not following a cause and I won't be hung under an umbrella of misconstrued principles!"

"Oh, very nicely put. I see you haven't lost your touch." Will wasn't put off, "You have no need of a man?"

"No, I do not!" She almost glared at him, "I can manage perfectly well on my own. This smacks of male chauvinism, Will. You!"

"Now who's labelling?"

Lyddy stuck to her guns, "Man's belief in the superiority of man. What else are you advocating?"

Will calmly watched her. His features quite deadpan now, he said, "Well, *I* have always admitted a preference."

"That's not what you meant and you know it!"

"Don't you think you're being a little over-sensitive?"

"No, I do not!"

Will grinned at her, "What about sheer pleasure then? What about man's belief in the essentiality of sex? Or woman's, in this case," he added lightly, as an afterthought.

She looked at him almost crossly. He was being too glib for comfort. "Are you winding me up?"

"Never. In a million years."

"Oh, I see. Very funny."

He slapped his hand on hers to grab it, "This takes me back. I'd almost forgotten what you were capable of."

Lyddy stared at him; he was enjoying this. She wouldn't let him off the hook that easily – she was still fired up. "You said the words. You intimated that feminism is defined by a woman's rejection of man. How could *you* get drawn into that? That's not what it's about. This is why I don't want to be cast under the label, because the word is misused. I can't be comfortable with it."

Will grinned again, "You always were easy prey for a wind-up."

He'd got her on the defensive now. She said, "Well! You were sounding like a real conformist twit back there!"

"It's hard to resist dangling the bait. You always snap it up so eagerly."

"And you were very convincing!"

"That's my job."

"Stop laughing at me!"

"More of an inward smile, my love."

"That's worse." She looked at him pointedly, she had to get her own back. "What are you doing here, anyway?" she asked. "Didn't you have anything to do this evening? Did you think, Oh, I know, I'll go and wind Lyddy up? That'll be good for a laugh."

"No," Will said lightly, "I didn't think of it till I got here!"

She gave him her best withering look, "Isn't it your bedtime, or something?"

Will laughed now, "Calming down, are we?"

"No, we're not."

"Never did know how to retreat with grace, did we?"

Lyddy had to grin at that, feeling a little foolish, but she had to hold on to some dignity, "I'm pleased to say that was never one of my strengths."

"You can say that again."

She narrowed her eyes at him, "And I'm still not convinced that your comments were just a wind up."

Will got to his feet, "That's for me to know and you to ponder." He put his glass on the table and smiled at her, "Now I've had my fun I must go."

Lyddy got up from the sofa. "Oh, very entertaining for you. I'll get my revenge," she said.

"I've no doubt of that," he replied and put his arms out for a hug. "By the way," he told her, "I'm not really advocating a partner for life, you know."

"I'm glad to hear it." She grinned at him. She felt like a performing monkey who'd done all his tricks right.

"I just think the occasional romp between the sheets adds a little zest to life."

She laughed at herself again. "You're probably right. I can't be bothered, that's all."

Will feigned a pained look. "Oh, dear. We'll have to put an ad in the paper. Lost. One libido. If found, keep warm and contact owner immediately."

Lyddy made a face at him, "Go home. I can only take so much."

He kissed her cheek, "Right. Take care, my love. Kiss the kids for me. I'll see you soon. Ring me," he added. "We'll make a date. You can come and see us."

"Okay, I will," Lyddy said. "Now go and bother someone else." She got his coat from the kitchen and saw him out.

Locking the front door behind him, she mulled over the scene and smiled; she had gone a bit over the top. She decided to leave her work and go to bed. She piled her books near the front door so that she wouldn't forget them in the morning and went into the kitchen to do what she had to do.

Upstairs, she went into the children's room to check on them. Nikki had kicked her quilt off and lay curled in a ball trying to keep warm in her sleep. Lyddy pulled the quilt over her and kissed her forehead.

Peter stirred as she lifted his head to put his pillow back on the bed. She kissed his cheek and squeezed his hand and kept the door ajar as she left the room to get herself ready for bed.

Chapter Four

"Mmm... pasghetti bolognese. My favourite." Nikki leant over to peer into the dish from which Chris was serving.

"Is it? That was a lucky choice then, wasn't it?" Chris passed a plate of food to her. "Peter?" She looked at him, "I hope you like pasghetti?"

"Yes, please, I love it. Nikki always says it wrong. She can't say it properly."

"Yes, I can. I just don't want to."

Lyddy mentally crossed her fingers. She had reminded them that morning to behave themselves at the meal table at Chris's. Meals at home seemed to be a bit chaotic these days, and she could only pray they would show some decent table manners when they were out. She hoped that most of the spaghetti would find its way into their mouths without making too much mess. It was hard for anyone to eat it with much decorum.

"Mummy says we can have a rabbit," Peter directed this information at Chris as he started collecting food on his fork.

"I can have a rabbit, you mean."

"Nikki! Don't start." Lyddy turned to Chris, "I shall have to check whether rabbits can be kept in a hutch together. I think we're going to have to get two."

"Hamsters eat each other if they're kept together, don't they, Mum?"

"Yes. Lovely while we're eating. Shall I cut that up a bit, Nikki?"

"No, I like it like this." Nikki gathered some long strands on her fork and held them in the air, her mouth open to catch the dangling ends.

Chris caught Lyddy's expression and laughed. "Nothing like spaghetti bolognese for getting in a mess. Don't worry, I'll probably make more mess than anyone."

Lyddy decided to ignore their eating habits and enjoy the meal. The children chattered on, hogging most of the conversation. They emptied their plates without too much mishap. Lyddy helped Chris clear the dishes and Chris brought a chocolate gateau to the table for pudding.

"Miss Carter? Can we play with Gertrude again after tea?" It was Peter's question.

"Yes, of course you can, but when we're out of school you can call me Chris."

Peter looked at her gravely.

Nikki looked surprised. "Is that your name?"

"It is. Did you think my mum had me christened Miss Carter?"

Peter looked at Lyddy for confirmation. She nodded her head, smiling.

"So we call you Chris when we're here," he said, always wanting to make sure he'd got the facts right, "but in school we call you Miss Carter?"

"Yes. You can manage that, can't you?"

"What if I forget?" said Nikki. "What if I call you Chris at school by mistake?"

"Well, you'll have to try to remember."

They both decided they could handle that and tucked into their pudding.

"I like it when someone else does the cooking for a change," Lyddy said.

"Well, actually, this is Sainsbury's best," Chris told her. "I'm not very good at puddings."

"Yes, but you know what I mean. Not to have to rush home and start cooking for once. I sometimes wish we didn't have to eat, all that shopping and cooking and clearing up. I'd like to be able to just pop a tablet in their mouths sometimes." Lyddy raised her eyebrows, "I'm probably an appalling mother to say such a thing."

Chris smiled. "I quite like cooking for other people. I can't always be bothered on my own."

"I help Mummy do the cooking, don't I, Mum?" Nikki put another spoonful in her mouth before she went on, "I help her make a cake sometimes."

"Nikki, finish speaking before you put more food in your mouth!"

Nikki put another mouthful in, "And I cut up things for salads, too."

Lyddy rolled her eyes, "Yes, darling, it's nice to have some help. We get it done in twice the time."

Nikki looked up, working it out, then saw that Lyddy was teasing her. "Well, I have to learn, don't I, Miss Carter... Chris?" She grinned self-consciously, using Chris's first name.

"Of course you do. Do you help, Peter?"

"Sometimes. I don't mind helping with the washing up. Mummy washes them and I dry them."

Lyddy scoffed light-heartedly, "If only! You sound as though you do it every day."

The children finished their pudding and went back out into the garden, putting their coats on as they went. It was still light. Chris got up and brought two cups of coffee in. She sat down pulling another chair closer and stretched her legs out on it.

"Aren't you glad it's Friday?" she said.

Lyddy leant back in her chair, pushing her hair into a bun with her hands as she spoke. She let it fall back onto her shoulders again. "Oh, absolutely. I don't have to get up in the morning and rush around." She paused. "Not that I get much of a lie-in at weekends but it's nice to get up and take things slowly, isn't it?"

"Too right. I was late for school this morning." Chris's face registered her annoyance with herself. "I slept through the alarm. I didn't wake up till half past eight."

"Did you have a late night?"

"I did, and I drank too much. I had a date, actually." She laughed at the memory.

Lyddy looked to see if she was going to elaborate.

"It was with this guy I used to be at university with. He lives around here and I bump into him occasionally. We've had the odd drink, you know." Her amusement still showed in her face. "Well, we went out for a meal last night. It was alright. We talked about people we knew at college, talked about our jobs, you know, usual stuff. We sat for ages, I drank far too much. Then," she looked at Lyddy, "he leant over the table and grabbed my hand. He was saying how much he'd enjoyed himself and did I want to go back to his place or mine. He thought we might as well go back to his place because it was closer and he started telling me about his water bed!"

"Oh, one of those. One of the presumptuous types. He provides the meal and you provide the services."

"Ha! We went halves on the meal. I certainly wasn't going halves on the services! Not with him, anyway. I said I had to go to the loo. I went to the Ladies and put some really pale make-up on my face. Then I went back to the table and told him I'd been sick. I said the food must have been too rich, I didn't think I'd got rid of it all yet and I'd better get home." Chris held her hand over her mouth, demonstrating. "You're a drama teacher – you would have been proud of me. I kept a straight face the whole time."

"Why didn't you just tell him you didn't want to go to bed with him?"

"I don't know. I was quite drunk; I just felt like winding him up. Anyway," she added, "he got me home double-quick. I didn't even have to think of an excuse why I didn't want to see him again. He didn't ask!"

Lyddy smiled as she said, "It's a long time since I had a date. I think I'd be very out of practice now, handling all that." Then she added, honestly, "I'm not really interested anymore, either."

"Well, I don't think you're missing much if last night was anything to go by." Chris was still tickled at the thought of it.

"A friend of mine keeps trying to fix me up but I've managed to avoid it so far." Lyddy looked wryly amused as she glanced at Chris. "Both he and my sister seem to think life can only go on if I'm partnered off." She paused. "Well, Annie won't be happy until she sees another husband safely installed in the little home." She grinned mischievously at Chris, "In Will's case, this friend, he doesn't have anything quite so long-term in mind. You know, just the odd night of passion now and then."

"He sounds like a practical chap."

"The essentiality of sex, he calls it."

"That depends who it's with, of course."

They sat chatting for a while longer, exchanging reminiscences of silly things that had happened on dates in the past. Lyddy was enjoying herself. She thought regretfully that she would have to get going soon. She looked at her watch; it was six thirty. She must get the children home. They would be getting cold outside as well.

She said apologetically, "We'll have to make a move. I'll help you clear up before we go."

"No, you won't. This is supposed to be your night off." Chris glanced out of the window at the children. "It's a shame you have to go."

Lyddy nodded. "They do rule your life a bit – the children, I mean."

Chris looked at her for a moment. "You should come round one evening, if you can get a baby-sitter. I'll rustle up something to eat and we can open a bottle."

Lyddy felt pleased at the offer. She liked Chris, liked her attitude to life. She could relax with her. It would be nice to be able to talk and enjoy herself without some other pressing demand on her.

"I'd like that," she said. She thought of her weekdays. "We'd better make it on a weekend, though, otherwise I'll fall asleep on you."

"Okay. Maybe next weekend."

Lyddy got up and opened the back door to call the children in. The sky was clear and the temperature had dropped considerably; there would be a frost tonight. The children must be freezing. They came into the kitchen, hands and faces red from the cold. She shouldn't have left them out for so long, but they didn't seem bothered. She followed them through to the sitting room where Chris was now kneeling by the grate, lighting a newly made up fire. She looked up as they came in.

"It's a bit of a fag, but I love it," she said.

They stood watching as the newspaper burned and the sticks of wood started to catch. Chris let the children put some small logs on. A pile of larger logs was stacked to the side.

"Can we have a log fire, Mum?" Nikki asked.

"It's lovely, isn't it?" Lyddy commented. "The trouble is, they take up time. You have to clean it out every day and lay it again."

"Nikki and I could do that," Peter said.

"Maybe when you're older."

They all sat back on their haunches watching the fire take hold, their faces reflecting the flickering light in the dim room. After a while, Lyddy reluctantly coaxed Nikki and Peter to their feet, reminded them to say thank you and herded them out into the chilly evening air. Chris saw them out to the car, leaning in to strap Nikki in for her. She waved as they drove off.

Chapter Five

The following Tuesday evening, Lyddy stood examining her face in the mirror, pleased with her findings. Her skin was looking good. She had lost weight since she started working full-time. It showed in the slight hollow under her cheek bones and she had noticed that the waistband of her jeans was looser too. She spied a grey hair reflecting the light and searched for it in her dark, wavy mass. She pulled it out.

Nikki and Peter were in the bath. They'd had the usual argument about whose turn it was at the tap end. Fortunately, the builder who'd had the house before Lyddy had put in a new bathroom to include a decent sized bath. Even so, she supposed they would have to bath separately before too long. They had a bath most nights. It quietened them down before bed and it saved time for them to get in together.

Lyddy picked up their discarded clothes in a bundle from the floor and went into their bedroom to sort them out, listening with one ear to Nikki singing a song she had learned in school. They started arguing about the words – Peter knew the song too. Lyddy let them carry on. It seemed an inevitable part of children growing up, to argue with their siblings. She used to think that it was only her children who argued so incessantly and couldn't help feeling that she was going wrong with them somewhere. She was more realistic about it now and other parents confirmed the same idiosyncrasy in their children. Bath time, of course, was more vulnerable than most because they were tired at the end of the day.

She became aware that the argument was developing into something more substantial, a splashing and tearful cries and the inevitable, "Mum!" Nikki, through her tears.

Lyddy went back into the bathroom to calm the situation. "Come on, Nikki, out you get. Peter, have you washed your face?"

"Mum! Peter kicked me!"

"Come on. Out you get. I'll tell you a story."

The ploy worked. They decided on the 'Princess and the Dragon'. It was her latest and one of her better ones, the dragon bursting from the forest breathing fire, declaring, "I'm hungry, I feel like a princess for my supper!" and the princess bursting from the castle, "No, I'm hungry, I feel like a dragon for my supper!"

Nikki loved these stories. She stood turning slowly, rapt, as Lyddy brushed her hair. They all joined in at the end as the princess was carried shoulder high into the castle, all the castle folk singing, "For she's a jolly good princess."

She sat with them on Peter's bed, one each side of her, leaning against the wall, Nikki curled up close, leaning her head on Lyddy's arm. Peter read some of his reader and Lyddy read them a story. After tucking them into bed, she went downstairs. She saw the lights of a car turn into the driveway and opened the front door. It was Annie, her sister. Lyddy stood waiting as Annie got out of the car, waved, and half disappeared into the back of the car. She emerged with a carrier bag full of something.

She was dressed in an immaculate, grey shell-suit and trainers, obviously on her way back from one of her keep-fit, yoga, aerobics or swimming sessions. Lyddy sometimes felt a stab of pity for her. She seemed to have joined the ranks of married women whose overriding occupation was to work their bodies at fever pitch at every opportunity. Lyddy felt it filled a gap. It filled their hours with a healthy occupation which denied censure. Annie didn't need to work; Bob earned a fortune and they had everything: immaculate home, cars of their choice, holidays without counting the cost. It would have been as inconceivable as it was unnecessary for Annie to work. So she filled her time. Not, Lyddy felt, out of guilt at her otherwise idleness, but simply that, to keep herself occupied.

Annie and Bob had desperately wanted children during the first years of their marriage. As they slowly gave up hope and dwelt on it less, Lyddy had hoped that Annie would conceive, as was often the case. But it didn't happen. In the circumstances, Annie had greeted the birth of first Peter and then Nikki with amazing charity and good grace. She idolised them both and welcomed any opportunity to fulfil her self-appointed role as second mum. Lyddy bore it with equanimity. The children loved her, lapped up the overt attention. In fact, since Lyddy had been on her own with them, she'd had many occasions to be grateful. She was never at a loss for a baby-sitter, providing Annie and Bob weren't throwing one of their lavish dinner parties. That was Annie's other life occupation.

Now, Annie stepped up to the front door. She was shorter than Lyddy, her fair hair short and impeccably styled. She was slightly built, her trimness attesting to her physical fitness. She proffered her cheek for a kiss and they hugged briefly.

"Hello, darling," Annie held out the carrier bag. "I've brought these for the children. There was a book sale at the Town Hall this morning. I'm afraid I went a bit mad."

Lyddy took the bag from her. It must have contained a dozen books, children's books.

"Thanks, Annie. I don't need to say it, do I?"

"I know, I spoil them," Annie said it for her.

Lyddy stepped back for her to come in and Annie went on, "I had an aerobics class tonight. I thought I'd drop them in on the way home. Bob's in Paris."

She was at an extra loss when Bob was away. Lyddy reflected gratefully, not for the first time, that at least Annie had a good marriage. They were one of the few long-married couples Lyddy knew of who still maintained a happy compatibility, and that after nearly twenty years.

"What's Bob doing?" Lyddy felt she should show some interest as she led the way to the kitchen. "Coffee or drink?" she asked before Annie could reply.

"Oh, drink please. Only one, I'm driving." Annie could hold her drink, unlike Lyddy, but she never overstepped the boundaries of what was proper or legal.

Lyddy poured them both a glass of wine while Annie chattered on, telling her about Bob's latest contract he was about to close on. They sat at the kitchen table. Lyddy was glad Annie had stopped by. Considering how different they were, as sisters they were close and Lyddy felt real affection for her.

"I thought I might just have caught the children up before they went to bed," Annie commented, obviously disappointed. "They must have been early tonight?"

"A little, they were tired."

"Dad didn't seem too bad at the weekend, did he?" Annie took a sip of her drink. She and Bob had come for Sunday lunch when her father had stayed the weekend at Lyddy's.

"No, I think it's getting easier for him, don't you? At least when he's here, he's side-tracked by the children."

At one time Lyddy had been worried about him, after her mum died, but suddenly, it seemed, he had started living again. He joined clubs, took up fishing, did up the house. It was just this time of year that was still a bit difficult, and Christmas, of course.

Lyddy topped up her glass and listened as Annie went on to talk about a mutual acquaintance, running her down somewhat.

She didn't live up to Annie's expectation of a responsible married woman; many people didn't. Annie could be very severe in her criticisms. She herself maintained an exacting high standard which would pass under anyone's scrutiny.

"You should have seen what she was wearing. Shopping in town! It looked like she'd gone through the cast-offs rejected by Oxfam."

"Annie, you are a snob." She would never have slopped around the supermarket in jeans and trainers as Lyddy often did.

"Well! And those children of hers. I don't think I've ever seen them without snot coming out of their noses. I think she washes their hair at Christmas and birthdays."

Lyddy laughed. She liked the woman in question but had to admit Annie did have some justification in her criticism this time.

"Well, I had to stop and talk to her. It would have been rude, wouldn't it? She held the baby up for me to see." Annie looked horrified, "I thought for a moment she was going to ask me to kiss it! Oh! You're invited to a party, by the way. Saturday. Their fifteenth anniversary or something. They're having fireworks in the garden." Her expression displayed her disapproval of their lack of taste. "I shan't go, of course. At least I had the excuse that Bob's away. She tried to get me to go on my own!"

Annie gabbled on and Lyddy suddenly remembered she needed a favour. Party. Saturday.

"Oh, Annie. Saturday. I can't go. In fact, I was going to ask you if you would baby-sit for me."

Annie stopped mid-torrent, unable to conceal her delight. "Of course, I will. Going anywhere nice?" Like Will, but for different reasons, she hoped to see Lyddy attached again at the earliest possible moment. It was, after all, well over a year now.

"Well, I'm having supper with Peter's teacher."

Annie looked at her, "How odd!"

Lyddy laughed tolerantly. "She's nice, fun; I enjoy her company. She takes the children home with her two days a week after school and I collect them from her house. We get on really well. She asked me to supper so I said yes."

"Is anyone else going?"

"No, I don't think so."

Annie clearly found it hard to contemplate such an evening as a social event. Really, she and Lyddy were miles apart. She still loved her dearly of course.

"Oh, well," she restricted herself to this without further comment. Lyddy was changing before her very eyes since David's death, a demise Annie secretly hadn't mourned, at least not on Lyddy's behalf. She had had to look on in pained frustration at Lyddy's apathetic misery during the last years of her marriage to David and couldn't imagine that things could have turned out better. But she didn't admit this to anyone, except Bob, and then she had only hinted at her thoughts. However, she found some of Lyddy's attitudes now genuinely baffling. She wasn't the least bit interested in finding anyone else.

Annie turned her thoughts towards Saturday and the children, "Anyway, why don't I have them over to stay for the night?" She felt the need to persuade Lyddy to agree, "They'll be company for me. Bob doesn't get back until Tuesday. And I'm not going to that damned party."

Lyddy was grateful. She didn't need persuading. "That would be great. They'll be pleased." They loved staying at Annie's, the large house, larger garden, even a small indoor swimming pool.

"Super," said Annie. "I'll think up something exciting to do with them on Sunday morning. You'll be able to have a lie in."

Lyddy had tried to explain on previous occasions that they were happy to spend their time in the pool or in the garden on nice days, but to no avail. Annie enjoyed treating them. She let it be. "Lovely," she said. "I'll bring them over, shall I? For tea?"

"No, I'm helping at the club on Saturday. I'll pick them up on my way home. About five?" The 'club', was formed of an elite band of businessmen and their wives. A general excuse to pat each other on the back and gloat, Lyddy thought, but that might be unfair.

"That would be fine," she answered.

Annie's demeanour altered subtly with this arrangement. She couldn't hide her pleasure in looking after the children. Lyddy felt the pity again, but she was grateful too. At least they all benefited.

Annie talked on for a bit longer, telling her about her plans for celebrating their twentieth wedding anniversary. Elaborate, expensive plans but nevertheless tasteful. It would be Annie's baby until the event.

She eventually got up to go, reaffirming the arrangements for Saturday. Lyddy went back into the kitchen and put the remains of the wine bottle in the fridge. The house always seemed strangely quiet after Annie had been.

Chapter Six

She arrived at Chris's just before eight. The children had gone off happily with Annie, leaving her with some time to herself. It was a luxury to get ready in peace, to have time for a leisurely bath and hair wash. She decided to stay casual, white jeans and a loose cotton shirt over the top.

She took a cab, leaving the car at home. It was less than a fiver each way so it was worth it. Chris opened the door before she knocked. She was dressed in a navy shirt tucked into a denim skirt, well above the knee, and navy tights. "I heard you coming. I was upstairs in the loo. Did you come in a taxi?"

"Yes, I hate not being able to drink." Lyddy passed the bottle she had brought to Chris and walked through the small hallway to the sitting room. It was lit by a lamp on the dining table and there was a warm glow around the fire. Lyddy breathed in curry and woodsmoke. "Mm... smells good."

Chris took her coat. "I'll get us a drink." She glanced at the fire, the red hot remains of logs not yet ashes. "You can do the fire for me if you like. It looks in need of a boost."

She went through to the kitchen and Lyddy knelt by the hearth. She poked about at the well burnt logs; ash which was spent fell through the bars of the grate onto the stone floor underneath. She picked out some suitable logs to put on the low blaze and thought how gratifying an open fire is. How it always attracted you to it, drew your eyes to it, moving, warming. She sat on the rug, moving herself backwards to lean against an easy chair close up to the fire.

Chris came back into the room with two glasses of wine. "The rice is on." She held out a glass.

"You must love living here." Lyddy took the drink offered, "Cheers. This room's so cosy and comfortable, isn't it?"

Chris settled into the armchair opposite, leant back and stretched her legs, moving them to one side to avoid Lyddy's. She nodded her head in agreement. "I do. It was the fireplace that sold the house. Well, actually, I don't own it. I found this place to rent while I looked around for somewhere to buy, but I like it here so much I've never been bothered to look very hard. Unfortunately, this isn't for sale. These cottages are owned by a land trust and they won't sell or can't sell, I'm not sure which." She leant forward and grabbed the poker to push the logs into a better position to burn. "To be honest, I'm never sure whether I want to buy or not. If you ever want to move it seems to be a horrendous nightmare, chains and gazumping and all that. As well as all those fees and taxes to pay."

"I don't blame you. I don't think I would want to move from here either. It's perfect. Mind you," Lyddy was looking around her, "it's not only the fire. The house we lived in before this one had an open fireplace but I wouldn't have called that warm and inviting. It was more of a show-piece mausoleum. We never even lit the fire – David said the smell would ruin the furniture."

Chris looked slightly bemused at this. Lyddy went on, a wry expression on her face, "I wasn't very happy there. It was David's house and somehow we all lived in it by David's rules." She glanced at Chris as she spoke, half apologetically; it seemed almost a sin now, looking back. "It was never a home. The children could only play in certain rooms in case the floorboards got scratched. The dog had to live in the utility room in case he messed up the rugs." She could have gone on but didn't want to dwell on it further.

Chris took the cue, realising now that maybe the marriage was not what it might have been. "I take it you've moved now."

Lyddy smiled, her features relaxed again. "Yes, when David died his life insurance paid off the mortgage but I didn't want to stay in the house. I sold it. Mind you," she added dryly, "the fire cheered it up a bit." She had started lighting the fire each evening. Dodger had loved it, he had the run of the house at last.

Chris gave a short laugh as she got up. "Come into the kitchen with me while I put the food out. Where did you move to?"

Lyddy told her the name of the road. She followed her through to the kitchen as she spoke. "It's a semi-detached, enough room but not too much, nothing grand but I love it." She leant in the doorway, watching Chris rinse the rice under the hot tap. "I feel happy there. The children like it." She wrinkled her nose, "It's never very tidy except when the cleaner's been, but it's home."

They took the plates of food and the bottle to the table and sat down. Chris moved the lamp onto the oak dresser, softening its effect. "You've got to be able to relax as you walk through your front door, haven't you?" she said. She topped up their glasses as she spoke.

"Absolutely, but I didn't realise how important that was until we moved into this house. Or maybe, more to the point, I hadn't realised at the time how awful it was in the other house."

Chris looked up from across the table, "It can't have been just the house though, was it?"

"No, of course not," Lyddy admitted. "The house just sticks out as a sort of symbol, I suppose."

She started telling Chris about David, his subtle dominance; his sullen, quiet periods which would last until he got his own way. Once things were running smoothly again for him he would go about life as though nothing had happened. It was as if he could totally exorcise his behaviour from his mind so that whenever Lyddy tried to talk to him about it he would look at her in impatient surprise, genuinely baffled by her frustrations. She had known this was all wrong; this wasn't how things should be, but she'd felt trapped in a bubble, unable to break out of his control.

He resented her friends; she had lost touch with many of them and was too embarrassed even now to try to patch up the long interval. He had considered them superfluous to her marriage. Of course, she hadn't seen for a long time what was going on right under her nose, and still apportioned some of the blame to herself. They even ceased seeing mutual friends to a large degree, friends they had made during their first years together. She supposed it was because the incentive to socialise as a couple faded as the relationship deteriorated. It became a pretence of maintaining the happy couple facade and there was no pleasure in it.

Lyddy had poured all her energies into the children to keep herself alive, so that life wasn't all cooking, cleaning, washing and ironing.

"It was a bloody way to live, wasn't it?" She smiled grimly as she finished her meal and reached for her wine. She looked at Chris, "I look back now with something between embarrassment and disgust, that I let things go that way."

Chris was contemplating all this. It was difficult to imagine, knowing Lyddy now. "You seem such a strong person," she said, "so sure of yourself."

Lyddy shrugged, she didn't understand it either.

"I hadn't realised that things had been like that – your marriage, I mean," Chris remarked. She raised her eyebrows, "I don't suppose you were alone. There are probably thousands out there right now still stuck in it all. I hate to say this but at least all that's over for you." She felt for Lyddy. She was glad it was over.

"Yes, well, that's been the difficult part to come to terms with, in a way." Lyddy leant back in her chair and clasped her hands behind her head as she explained, "I kicked him out, you know."

"No, I didn't," Chris shook her head, surprised.

"I did actually get to the point where I couldn't stand it any more. I didn't know what I was going to do but I told David that if he didn't go then I would take the children to my dad's." Lyddy allowed herself a small dry laugh, "He didn't believe me until he came home early the next day and I was packing. So he moved out. But to him it was only a temporary thing." She scoffed lightly, "I think he thought I was having a brainstorm or something, a nervous breakdown. He probably thought that if he did as I asked for a while, I would calm down and things would get back to normal."

"I didn't know that you split up before he died. What happened?" Chris's dark eyes were watching Lyddy as she took all this in.

Lyddy looked up. "His death? It was an accident. A bloody stupid, terrible accident." She didn't want the evening to go this way. It wasn't pleasant for her to dredge all this up but somehow she had wanted to tell Chris how things had been. She relaxed her expression and grinned across the table at her, "I'll tell you another time."

"Did you feel awful?" Chris imagined being in Lyddy's shoes at the time.

Lyddy made a final effort. "Yes, that was the hard part." She couldn't apologise, but it was difficult to own up even to herself. "I felt relief, and guilt of course. Guilt at this overwhelming feeling of relief. I'd been released. It was like being trapped on a loose ledge on the side of a cliff and being lifted to safety in the nick of time." She grinned at Chris, despite herself. "Good metaphor, typical English teacher." She thought, then grimaced, serious again. "Well, it was all over, just like that. It's hard to admit it still, but that's how it was." She breathed in deeply and let it out slowly. "Things started looking up in all respects after that. Life changed completely, for me and for the kids."

Chris felt guilty at having pushed her to talk about it.

"I'm sorry," she said, "I didn't intend to invite you round here to rake over unpleasant memories. I meant you to come and relax."

She stood up. "Shall we go and sit by the fire? We'll change the subject. I'll tell you about Bill, that'll make you laugh." She held up the empty bottle, "Do you want to change to something else or more of this?"

Lyddy pulled a face as she stood up, "I'd better stick to wine otherwise I'll have a hangover tomorrow." She laughed at herself, "I'll probably have a hangover anyway but it will be worse if I mix drinks."

Chris got another bottle from the kitchen and took it through to where Lyddy had knelt by the fire. She passed the bottle and a corkscrew to her. "Can you do this for me? It's got a cork. I'll be all night opening it and then we'll be spitting out the bits."

Lyddy opened the bottle and refilled the glasses which Chris brought over. She sat back against the sofa in front of the fire and watched while Chris poked at it, put another log on, then sat on the rug leaning against an easy chair.

"What was so funny about Bill?" Lyddy asked.

Chris's eyes shone in the firelight. "It will show my cruel side if I tell you about Bill. He was a bit of an old woman. I don't know how we lasted so long, really." She sipped from her drink while she wondered where to start, then put her glass on the stone surround of the fireplace. "I'll put some more music on first," she said.

Sitting by the fire, feeling its warmth, Lyddy started to feel blissfully content. She didn't have to worry about getting home for the baby-sitter; she didn't have to think about getting up with the children in the morning. She was glad she hadn't driven over – she was feeling the effect of the wine and enjoying it. She thought she would slow down on the booze, otherwise she'd start slurring her words.

She was enjoying Chris's company. She felt completely relaxed with her, feeling she didn't have to watch what she said. She could tell her anything. She didn't have to tone down her language if she broke into the occasional curse. She had always felt like this with Will. He had always been unshockable and uncensoring.

Chris told her about Bill, his idiosyncrasies. He was a person of routine, everything had to be done in the right order. She made Lyddy laugh over his bedtime routine.

He was not a spontaneous person; everything had to be planned and executed according to the plan. He was a worrier, particularly over his job. He had been made Head of Department at his school and the pressure had sometimes been too much. He used to come home and pour out his worries to Chris, minute details of who said what and when. How he thought he would tackle the problems. Most of it, she said, was not of interest to her. Most of it, she thought, should have been dealt with as a matter of course by anyone with sufficient self-confidence to take on a Head of Department's job.

Lyddy thought of some of the teachers she had known and knew. She laughed derisively, "I thought those were the required qualities for Head of Department," she said, "self-doubt, lack of imagination, no self-esteem."

Chris was amused by her mocking, "Goodness, you don't think much of teachers, do you?"

Lyddy shrugged her shoulders resignedly. "It's secondary school, isn't it? I don't know why." She relented a little, "I go a bit overboard, I suppose. It's not totally rife, I know that, but secondary schools do seem to have their fair share of bumbling, boring old farts, don't they? I'm sure they didn't all start that way." She added lightly, "I might end up like it after a few more years."

Chris smiled, she didn't think so. "I think with Bill, it became a matter of survival. He had desperately wanted the job and then found he wasn't really up to it. That was probably when I started seeing him in a new light. He became a bit of a waste of space in my life." She grinned, "You see, I told you it would show my cruel side."

They chatted on, finishing the bottle. Chris drank more than Lyddy; she could obviously hold her drink. They laughed at some of the amusing anecdotes which accumulate working in a school. They got on to embarrassing moments. Lyddy told her about the time she had whipped a tissue out of her skirt pocket to stifle a sneeze. She had been talking to the whole class at the time, had their undivided attention. With the tissue came a Tampax which she had put in her pocket to use at break time.

"It flew across the room like a white torpedo and landed on someone's desk." The memory of it still made Lyddy laugh.

"Oh, my God! What did you do?"

"Well, it was a class of fifteen year olds. There was a silence you could have cut with a knife and then I grinned and there was uproar. Everyone laughed. I did too. I dashed over and stuffed it back in my pocket quick."

Chris was laughing with her. Lyddy added, "Some bright spark shouted, 'What's that for then, Miss?' winding me up."

"I suppose it was all round the school by lunchtime."

"Well! I was making a coffee in the staffroom later and the deputy head came up and said very quietly, you know, very dryly," she mimicked his tone, 'Don't you use a handbag, Lyddy?' She looked over at Chris, "Needless to say, I do now."

Laughing, Chris got up to put some more music on. "Do you fancy some coffee, or shall I open another bottle?"

Lyddy stretched and pushed her shoes off. "No, I'm feeling slightly tipsy," she said. "I'd better have some coffee."

Chris put another CD on and went into the kitchen. Lyddy leant against the sofa, her knees drawn up slightly so that her feet rested flat on the floor, feeling happy, listening to the music. It was Van Morrison, 'Tupelo Honey'.

When Chris came back with the coffee she sat down beside Lyddy. "Have a chocolate. A present from my neighbours for looking after the guinea pig."

They sat there, digging into the chocolate box, drinking their coffee, looking into the fire, a comfortable lull in the conversation. The effect of the fire, the wine and the music was soporific.

After a while, Lyddy said peacefully, "I love your fire, it's very calming." She turned her head to look at Chris's profile and back again to the fire, "I can't remember when I last felt so relaxed."

They both giggled as Chris said, "I'll nudge you if you drop off."

Neither of them spoke again for a time. Lyddy sat contentedly gazing into the fire, mesmerised by its glowing movement, the flames flickering around the burning wood. A log slipped as its red-hot underside disintegrated in the heat.

She became aware that Chris was watching her and turned her head. Chris had half turned towards her, resting her arm on the seat of the sofa, looking at her intently, solemnly. "Lyddy?" She spoke quietly.

"Hm?"

"Have you ever kissed a woman?"

Lyddy smiled slightly, the question was unexpected. "No, I haven't," she answered. "Have you?"

"No." Chris didn't take her eyes off her.

Lyddy studied Chris's face in the firelight. She was very attractive, dark hair, brown eyes, lovely cheek bones, a sort of radiance about her in this light. She was looking back at Lyddy, into her eyes, obviously in some indecision. Then she said, almost breathed, "Can I kiss you?"

Lyddy didn't recoil or panic. Her face didn't alter its expression. The wine, the warmth and the music had tranquillised her to such an extent that she wasn't shocked. To her surprise she felt flattered. She absently wondered whether her liking of Chris had been influenced by some other attraction, but didn't know.

She focused again on Chris who was sitting quietly, waiting for her to reply, those lovely eyes still watching her. She decided to be reckless. "Yes," she said softly, and allowed a small smile, "I won't run off into the night."

"No, I didn't think you would."

Chris looked at Lyddy for a few moments longer and Lyddy half turned towards her, aware of a mild flutter in her chest.

Chris leant forward and touched her lips to Lyddy's, holding them there, then pulled back gauging her reaction. Lyddy didn't move. Now she was watching Chris's face, waiting, frozen in expectation.

Chris reached to put her free hand behind Lyddy's neck under her hair and pulled her towards her and kissed her again, softly, but this time pushing Lyddy's lips apart with her tongue.

Somewhere in her mind Lyddy registered that she was aroused by it. She pulled her face away slowly, Chris's hand still clasping her neck.

"My God!" Lyddy murmured.

Chris's hand pulled Lyddy towards her once more and they kissed again, mouths open now, their tongues touching, softly, gently. Lyddy pushed her mouth harder onto Chris's in response. It lasted a full minute. Lyddy hadn't felt like this for a long time. It was a long-forgotten sensation, one from her past.

Lyddy's left arm leant on the sofa, her other hand resting in her lap, their only contact being where their mouths met and Chris's hand on her neck. It ended and they both came back for more.

When they drew apart Chris let her hand drop. Lyddy shifted her position slightly to bend her legs, one under the other on the floor, keeping her eyes on Chris. She wondered who was going to speak first, wanting this moment to last.

"You're lovely," murmured Chris, her eyes moving over Lyddy's face.

Lyddy leant her cheek on her hand, her elbow on the sofa. This wasn't over yet. She suddenly felt very sober. She spoke quietly, "This has taken me totally by surprise, you know."

Chris allowed a small smile of acknowledgement but she didn't speak.

"Did you plan this?" Lyddy paused. "To seduce me in front of the fire?"

"No, I don't know what I planned." She shook her head and grinned, a little shy now.

They were both keeping their voices low, just loud enough to hear each other above the music in the background.

Lyddy wanted to understand. "You took a risk, didn't you? I could never have done what you did."

Chris raised her eyebrows a little. "It was rather on impulse. Impetuous, you see. If I'd thought about it for too long I wouldn't have done it." She watched Lyddy, waiting for her to speak again.

Lyddy remained silent, studying Chris's face, her cheek still leaning on the palm of her hand. Then she said, "I'm glad you did." A gentle smile slowly covered Chris's face, starting with her eyes and ending with her mouth. Lyddy went on, still speaking softly, "It's a bit scary though, isn't it?" She was waiting now for what would happen next.

Chris nodded. "Yes," was all she said. They sat silent for several seconds without taking their eyes off each other. Lyddy could feel her heart banging away as she looked back. The moment was too much for her; she wanted the physical contact again. She lifted her hand from her lap to hold Chris's head as she pressed her open mouth on to hers. As they kissed, Chris pulled Lyddy up so that they were both kneeling, their bodies touching. She put her arms around Lyddy's waist, slipping them up inside her shirt loose over her jeans, to feel the bare skin of her back.

Lyddy felt light-headed at the touch and wrapped her arms around Chris's neck. The kiss ended but they kept their lips apart, touching, and she could feel the rise and fall of Chris's breathing. She felt excited, nervous, aroused, all in one. Then Chris gently pulled her over on to her back on the rug by the fire. Lyddy didn't resist; she had a need in her now. She felt she was on a roller coaster; couldn't stop it and didn't want to.

Chris lay along the side of her, leaning on her elbow, and raised her head to focus on Lyddy's eyes. Lyddy looked up at her, watching her face in the firelight, meeting her eyes again. She had an absurd thought and nearly giggled: Found, One Libido. She put her hand up to run it through Chris's hair as Chris undid each button on Lyddy's shirt, feeling her way, looking at Lyddy all the while. Lyddy pulled out Chris's shirt and rubbed her hand over the warm, soft skin underneath. She closed her eyes and Chris bent to kiss her again. Lyddy felt a wave of physical longing wash through her body as Chris lay half on top of her and started running her mouth over her neck.

It was nearly three in the morning when Lyddy got home.

She went straight upstairs. She could hear Dodger scuffling excitedly at the kitchen door but didn't go in to see him. She brushed her teeth, piled her clothes in a heap on a chair, closed off the turmoil of thoughts going through her mind and was asleep within minutes of getting into bed.

Chapter Seven

The next evening, Lyddy stood on the landing leaving the children's door ajar. Peter wouldn't sleep in the dark. Quite confident in some ways and yet so nervous in others. Nikki, on the other hand, had few terrors. The day would come when she would have to put them in separate rooms. At eight or nine she'd read somewhere, girls and boys should no longer share a bedroom.

"Night, Mum!" Peter's voice called out, aware that she hadn't yet gone downstairs. "I love you!"

"Good night, sweetheart," she called softly. "Love you. Go to sleep now."

"See you in the morning," he called, always wanting the last word.

"Alright, my love." She stood still, listening to the quiet, wondering what to do. Ironing, pay the bills, marking? No, none of those. She needed a drink. A dozen things to do and no incentive to do any of them. A soak in the bath with a gin and tonic, she decided. She couldn't put it off any longer. She had to think.

She went downstairs into the sitting room and started putting toys away, except for Peter's castle. It was almost finished. He rarely finished things, but improvised, when he started getting fed up with something, to bring it to a fast conclusion. His latest creation looked as though it was in with a chance. It was looking very castle-like.

Kneeling by the stereo, putting stray bits of Lego in the box, she switched it on and pressed the CD start button wondering what had been left in there. Pachelbel cruised out of the speakers. Canon in D major. She sighed, drinking it in. Her favourite piece of music in the world. If you got together all the people in the world who professed this to be their favourite, what would the psychologists and analysts make of them? Probably manic depressives, she decided. But it's so beautiful, she involuntarily defended herself.

All the toys put away, she started to get up to go and run the bath. The phone rang. Settling onto the arm of a chair she picked it up. "Hello?"

"Lyddy."

She felt an absurd pleasure at the sound of the voice. "Chris," she responded. What would she say? Calmly ask, "How are you?" She had been putting all thoughts of last night to the back of her mind to address them and deliberate at her leisure, when she felt ready. She had consigned that task to the bath.

Chris asked, "How are you?" Concerned, not quite sure of the response she was going to get. She was apologetic, honest and open, "I tried not to phone but I had to. I've been in a bit of a state all day. Can I see you?"

Lyddy herself had been in 'a bit of a state' all day. "I'm fine," she answered the easiest part first. Not true, she thought. "Knackered, actually. Late night, last night."

"Yes, me too."

Lyddy grinned. She said, "I was just going to take a gin and tonic into the bath."

Chris waited at the other end of the line.

"Come round," Lyddy offered, deliberately not giving herself time to think. "But no hanky-panky," she added, keeping her tone light, "with my children upstairs in bed."

Chris laughed. "I'll be about half an hour," she said. "I've got to drop some stuff off at a friend's. I'll do it on the way."

"Okay," said Lyddy. "Well, I'll have my bath anyway. I'll leave the back door unlocked in case I'm still upstairs when you come." She trusted Dodger to warn her of any unwanted callers. "It's number thirty," she added, remembering that Chris hadn't been to the house before.

"See you in a bit." The line went dead.

Lyddy put the phone down and stared intently at it.

Oh God! "Calm down, Lydia."

She ran her forearm absently along the bookshelf as she walked out of the room. The dark wood always showed the dust. It came off in a line along the bottom edge of her sleeve and she brushed it off. Mrs Page would sort it out in the morning. She went through to the kitchen and unlocked the back door.

"Forever young, I want to be forever young," she sang softly to herself as she went upstairs to run her bath and hummed the rest of the song wondering whether to have the gin and tonic after all. It would just be Dutch Courage, she thought, and she settled on a large one.

She decided that the gin and tonic in the bath warranted a copious amount of foam bath. She lay back, luxuriating in the silky-soft water, deep enough to cover her toes as she lay with her legs outstretched. She glanced up at the Mickey Mouse clock on the shelf, a present from Peter at Christmas. They had reached the age when they wanted to choose their gifts themselves. Half past eight. She had about quarter of an hour to soak and then she'd make a move. She wanted to be out and dressed when Chris arrived.

Lyddy took a sip of her drink and forced herself to analyse her feelings. She knew why she hadn't let herself think about what happened last night. She knew that she had no decisions to make. They had been made for her. She had enjoyed last night, had no regrets. In fact, she had more than enjoyed it. She fancied another woman, had had sex with her, and was trying to contain her excitement at the thought of seeing her again. Why should I want to contain my excitement, she thought. Because I haven't adjusted to it yet. The body has, the brain's got to catch up.

She hadn't stayed all night at Chris's because she hadn't been sure how she was going to feel when she woke up in the morning, and had wanted to do so in her own bed. Chris had understood, hadn't tried to dissuade her.

In fact, when she did wake up and the memory flooded back she had to admit that it was greeted with a mixture of elation and panic. Well, I know why the elation, she thought. Now the panic. The implications she couldn't avoid, the 'what-would-people-think': her Dad, Annie… oh, my God, the children. Not yet. This is going too fast, she decided, relieved to put away such thoughts for the moment. One thing at a time.

She was aware that she felt a physical thrill at the thought of seeing Chris again and, she had to admit, a little nervousness. It wasn't only that she found herself attracted to another woman. This was strange territory to her these days; she hadn't considered another person in this way for such a long time. She discovered that she was enjoying it, the anticipation.

Lyddy's thoughts were broken by the phone ringing again.

"Oh, bloody hell!" she muttered and pulled herself up out of the water.

She quickly dried her legs and feet so she wouldn't drip everywhere and wrapped a large towel around her, tucking it in under her armpits. She grabbed the remains of her drink and made for the bedroom, the phone on the bedside table. "Yes?" She was sharp but sometimes couldn't help herself when the phone rang inconveniently.

"Lyddy. I hate it when you answer the phone like that."

Lyddy relented. "Hello, Will. I'm sorry, I can't help it. Sometimes the phone just intrudes, doesn't it? Anyway, how are you? Still busy, I suppose?" She plumped up the pillows on the bed and lay back, propped up on them, phone held between cheek and shoulder, drink in hand.

"I've been really bogged down," Will said. "We've been preparing this assault case. We're in court on Monday."

"How's Carl? Have you seen him lately?" A pointed dig at their busy workloads.

"Very funny. He's fine. He sends his love. In fact we're going to have a holiday when this case is finished. I'm owed loads of time. Carl's got a manager starting next month. He'll be able to take some time off as well."

"Good. It's what you both need."

"When are you coming over to see us?" Will went on. "You haven't been over here for ages. Get a baby-sitter, get a cab and come and get drunk. I'll invite that chap at work I was telling you about." Will, trying to fix her up again.

"No, don't do that. I might bring someone." Oh, God, that was a little impetuous.

"Aha! You have a lover. I thought you were done with all that."

"Yes, well..." she left it deliberately open.

"Just what I've been prescribing. Tell me."

Lyddy stalled. She was adamant. "No, mind your own business." They both laughed.

"Come on," Will wanted to know. "What's his name?"

His use of the masculine pronoun. Her heart gave a flutter, a real physical feeling, her first test. If she failed with Will she had no chance with anyone else.

She failed. She wasn't ready. She continued to play for time. At least in this case she could answer without compromise; it would give nothing away anyway. "Chris," she said.

"Okay. Chris." She heard Will take a deep breath. He started winding her up, knowing all the while that she wouldn't tell him until she was ready.

"Where did you meet him? How old is he? What does he do? Does he make you laugh? Does he flick his fingers at the waiter?"

"Very droll." This was a reference to David.

Will affected a serious tone, "Do you know each other intimately?"

Lyddy laughed this time. "Mind your own bloody business. You will have to wait," she intoned the words deliberately, spacing each, talking through her grin.

She took a gulp of her now warm gin. She was enjoying this. Holding the phone in one hand she glanced round to look at the clock on the bedside table, aware that the minutes were ticking by.

Chris was leaning in the doorway, hands in coat pocket, watching her with those lovely eyes.

Lyddy grinned, keeping her eyes on Chris, a racy flutter in her chest again. I hope my heart's strong, she thought, or I'll peg out before I get much enjoyment out of this.

"Will, I've got to go, my darling. I'll see you soon. I'll ring you." She still had her head turned looking at Chris, savouring the moment. She's gorgeous, she thought.

Chris remained where she was, her eyes still on Lyddy, smiling.

"You rarely ring me." Will's tone was matter of fact. He always said Lyddy was the world's worst at getting on the telephone, except when there was an emergency. "He's there, isn't he?" he said. "Can I pop round?"

"No, you can't. I love you. I'll see you soon, really."

"Bye, my darling. Enjoy yourself."

Lyddy put the phone back on its cradle, still watching Chris. She glanced quickly down at herself, dressed only in the bath towel. She made a face, looking back at Chris. "I had good intentions," she said. "I was going to be out of the bath and dressed before you got here. I got side-tracked." She inclined her head slightly towards the phone and back in explanation.

Chris straightened up and walked over to her. She sat on the edge of the bed against Lyddy's thigh. "So I see," she said with a smile. Then she asked, "Who was that?" Lyddy had just said 'I love you', down the phone.

Lyddy's affection for Will showed in her voice. "That was my best friend in the world. His name's Will. He's what everyone should have – my confidante, guardian angel and emotional sponsor all rolled into one." She put her head on one side as she made her admission, "There are times when I don't think I would have managed without him." She remembered, fleeting thoughts of the awful times towards the end of her marriage and after David's death. Will had been wonderful.

Chris's smile faded now. She waited for Lyddy to speak again, searching her face for some sign.

Lyddy suddenly realised Chris's uncertainty and hesitation, that she wasn't taking anything for granted. After all, Lyddy had told her that she didn't know how she was going to feel in the cold light of day. She now reflected that Chris still didn't know how she felt. She put her drink down on the bedside table and took Chris's hand, smiling, watching her face. She glanced at the open door. Peter rarely woke during the night; he virtually went into a coma for the first part of it. Nikki always called out on the rare occasions that she woke; she never got out of bed.

"Push the door to," Lyddy said. No need to be too daring.

Chris did so, and sank back in her position on the bed. She reached over Lyddy to rest one hand across her on the bed.

Lyddy looked at her, aware that she was waiting. She took her hand again. "It's alright," she said with a gentle smile, then laughed shortly at herself, "more than alright."

Chris's expression relaxed. Neither moved for a few moments. Lyddy studied Chris's face. She was so attractive, those lovely eyes. Chris leant over and touched Lyddy's lips with her own and started to pull back. Lyddy raised her hand and pulled the back of Chris's head down towards her. They kissed again, but this time lips, tongues, lasting forever.

Then Chris drew away a little and put both arms around the back of Lyddy's neck so that their faces were close. "I didn't know what to expect. I'm so glad," she said softly. She grinned self-consciously. "It's a bit out of character for me, to feel like that. I couldn't handle it."

In answer, Lyddy reached inside Chris's coat and slid both arms around her.

Chris added, good-humouredly, "You obviously didn't have the same problem."

Lyddy's features broke into an apologetic smile. It was true. It hadn't occurred to her to doubt Chris's feelings the morning after. She had only been concerned with facing up to her own. She said, "You're a wonderful kisser. I've never felt weak at the knees before when I've been lying down."

Chris laughed. She bent her head to look down at where Lyddy's towel had come untucked at the top. "I think we should get off this bed and go downstairs. With your children asleep in the house – what would Peter think if he found me here?"

Lyddy sighed and brought her legs up to wrap them around Chris. The towel slipped off further. They kissed again, for a long time. "Okay," Lyddy said at last. "You move first. You're probably the stronger willed. I'll follow. In fact, I'll throw some clothes on to show my good intent."

Chris got off the bed as Lyddy swung her legs over the side and stood up, leaving the towel behind. Chris put her hands on Lyddy's bare hips and pulled her towards her so that their bodies touched. "You are lovely. This isn't fair," she murmured.

"I know." Lyddy laughed, pushing Chris's coat off her shoulders onto the floor and wrapping her arms around her again. "Shall we make it fair?"

Chris rubbed her hands over Lyddy's back and down to her bottom. She pressed her face into Lyddy's bare shoulder and heaved a sigh, thinking of the children asleep in the next room. Then she looked up. "No, I haven't got the bottle," she said reluctantly. "You're shameless. Put some clothes on." Then she added, with determination, "*I'm* going downstairs."

Lyddy laughed again as Chris picked her coat up and walked towards the door.

Chapter Eight

Lyddy padded into the kitchen on bare feet. She had put on an old, baggy grey sweatshirt and leggings and brushed her hair out of the bun she'd had it in for her bath. Chris straightened up from making a fuss of Dodger who stood looking up at her for more attention, tail wagging. Her features broke into a smile at Lyddy, dressed again.

"I see you and Dodger have made friends," said Lyddy. "He didn't even bark when you came in." Checking the kettle had water in it, she switched it on and she leant against the worktop, standing close to Chris. She put her arm comfortably around Chris's waist.

"Dodger. Why did you call him Dodger?"

"Because his ancestry was largely unknown, dodgy."

"He's lovely. He's got character."

"Yes, he's definitely got that." Lyddy turned round to put coffee in two mugs as she spoke.

They went into the sitting room. Chris sat on the sofa, angled into the corner of it, slightly sprawled. Dodger followed them in, tail wagging slowly, and sat with his head on Chris's knee. Lyddy put the mugs on the low table and walked over to the stereo. She thought of pressing the start button on Pachelbel again but decided against it. That was solitary music. She searched through the CDs and chose Mary-Chapin Carpenter, something more cheerful. She picked up her mug and settled herself on the middle seat of the sofa with her legs curled under, close to Chris.

They grinned at each other, at the situation they found themselves in. Chris had more than regained her normal self-confidence, her features reflecting her wry amusement. "Bit of a turn-up for the books, ain't it?" she said.

"Indeed!" Lyddy answered dryly. "I shall be more wary next time I blithely accept an invitation to supper." She felt absurdly pleased that Chris was there now, that things had turned out this way.

Chris obviously felt the same. She took Lyddy's hand and held it, rubbing her thumb affectionately over the back of it. "I'm glad you did accept," she said.

A thought occurred to Lyddy. "Was your invitation totally innocent?" she asked. "Did you think about this? Before last night, I mean."

Chris looked at her for a moment. "Fleetingly," she admitted. Her smile broadened a little at her confession.

"Did you, really? How fleetingly?"

"Well, several times." She laughed.

"Well, I had no chance then, did I?" Lyddy liked Chris's candid honesty and her capacity to laugh at herself. "Have you fancied women before?"

Chris rolled her eyes, "Oh, no! The inquisition."

Lyddy gave a short laugh, "No, it's not. I'm interested."

"Yes, occasionally. Fleetingly." Chris grinned. "It's still come as a bit of a surprise, though."

"Yes, I'll go along with that. But a pleasant one."

Chris leant over to put her mug back on the table and held Lyddy's hand in both of hers. "I was in a total stir all day. I woke up this morning and couldn't believe last night. I felt wonderful," grinning at herself. "Then the doubts and anxieties took over. I thought you would wake up embarrassed or shocked or God knows what. I thought you would be ringing me with excuses why I needn't take the children home with me any more." She looked at Lyddy, with a rueful expression, "So that you didn't have to see me again. This was all new to me, this failing of my confidence. You had the advantage on me."

Lyddy smiled and said, "I have to admit, I didn't let myself think about it all day, until you phoned." She was apologetic, "I can do that, stuff things away until I'm ready for them. It always annoyed David, especially when I could empty my mind and fall asleep instantly after some particularly trying scene with him." It was a trait she was often grateful for. It had helped her through many not so good times, but she also felt it was something of a fault, a head-in-the-sand attitude.

"You shouldn't apologise for it. You're lucky. I barely got through the day. I needed to see you, but I didn't want to be pushy." Chris scoffed at herself. "I felt like a teenager and I felt a bit stupid.

I'm thirty-five and I was behaving like a sixteen year old. I even left the answer phone on all day and just listened as people left messages." She laughed, "Except, of course, I would have answered it like a shot if you had phoned, which you didn't!" Her good humour came through the accusation.

Lyddy put her empty mug on the floor and turned herself round to sprawl on the sofa next to Chris, head on her shoulder. She kissed Chris's cheek and looked up at her, thinking of the children. They were a responsibility that she never regretted or cursed. They were simply part of her life now. "I wish you could stay. It's going to be a bit like this. Can you handle it?" She was aware of the implication of her words, reference to the future, that they were going somewhere, that this wasn't an overnight fling.

Chris turned her face to Lyddy. She pulled her arm out from under Lyddy to put it around her and pressed her lips to Lyddy's forehead. "Yes, I can. Well, I'll do my best." Then she looked thoughtful and seemed to make up her mind. "Lyddy, there's something I ought to tell you. I wasn't going to tell anyone; I was going to see how it goes. It might come to nothing."

"Is this a riddle?"

"I applied for another job, weeks ago, deputy head near Oxford. I have an interview on Thursday." It would mean moving house, living eighty miles away.

It reflected Chris's feelings towards Lyddy that she felt obliged to tell her of the interview. Lyddy felt happy at the inference. "And leave your lovely fireplace?" She kept her tone light. The possible consequences were too far in the future to think about now.

She studied Chris's face, close up. "I'm glad you told me. You'll probably get the job." Chris had a reputation at the school. She was enthusiastic in her job, her temperament suited to dealing with thirty seven year olds for six hours a day. She always had time for their jokes or tears, or their struggles when they needed a bit of extra help or coaxing. She was always positive with them, encouraging.

Lyddy added, "My father lives near Oxford." Despite herself, she felt faintly unsettled but pushed any such thoughts from her mind. It was early days. Instead, she said, "You'll have to watch what you say. Do they ask you about your personal life? 'Do you have a... er... um partner, Miss Carter?' 'Well, yes, actually, her name's Lydia.'" Lyddy pulled a face at her own sense of humour.

Chris smiled at her then thought for a moment. "God knows what my mum and dad would say." About her and Lyddy.

Lyddy felt a moment of panic but forced herself to be rational. She put her arm across Chris's waist and squeezed her. "You're in your mid-thirties. I don't think what your parents say matters all that much." She raised her eyes to glance up at Chris, adding facetiously, "Brave words, Lydia." She didn't want to dwell on that. At the moment she was happy. "Don't think about it," she said. "One day at a time."

Chris shot her impish look. "Maybe the odd night at a time as well." They both giggled.

They lay sprawled, talking on, happy to be together, enjoying each other's company, adjusting to this sudden change in their lives. Lyddy reflected how happy she was to be with Chris, how long it was since she had felt like this.

The music came to an end and Lyddy got up to put some more on. She chose another CD and put it on, turning down the volume a little. "Do you want some more coffee? Or something else?"

"Another coffee would be fine. I drank too much last night and look where that got me." Chris followed Lyddy into the kitchen and looked around as Lyddy made the coffee: the large room, fitted wooden units all round, thick cushioned lino on the floor, big pine table in the middle, double glazed stained wood windows. "I like the house, Lyddy. It's bigger than I imagined."

Lyddy was pleased. "I bought it from a builder; he'd spent five years doing it up. Fortunately, he had a wife with good taste. Sometimes builders go a bit over the top, don't they, doing up their homes."

"I think it's lovely. Warm and friendly."

Lyddy smiled with satisfaction. "It's mine," she said. "David wouldn't have approved. It wouldn't have been big enough or grand enough." She put the coffees on the table and leant against a kitchen cupboard, across the table from Chris.

"You were going to tell me what happened when he died," Chris said, looking at Lyddy to see if this was the right moment.

Lyddy took a deep breath and let it out slowly, wondering whether she wanted to talk about it now. She decided she would. "It was one of those freak accidents," she stopped, thinking how to get over the feeling, "that sets you wondering what it's all about. Why do we bother? It makes everything seem so pointless."

"What happened?" Chris asked gently.

Lyddy stared at Chris for a few moments, wondering where to start. Telling it meant reliving it but she wanted to tell her. It wasn't only David's death, it was the end of her marriage, that part of her life. "It was three weeks after David moved out. Everything was in a mess. He was staying at a friend's flat. This guy had gone to America for a year so his flat was empty. But David insisted on seeing this as a temporary measure, to 'give me time'." She grimaced, "I just couldn't get through to him that it was over. I didn't know what I was going to do. I didn't feel I could stay in the house because it was David's house and always would be to me. I only had a part-time job and I couldn't just move out with the children. Where to? I didn't have any spare money. We lived well but every penny had to be accounted for." She paused, thinking back.

"I felt so worn out. Just keeping alive had been hard work. I had a breathing space with him gone but I felt so panicky to do something before he decided it was time to move back." Her gesture was a hopeless one, to indicate the quandary she had felt herself in. "I just couldn't see the wood for the trees. Meanwhile, David was turning up out of the blue. He'd call in after work on his way back to the flat and sit around like a house guest. He would try to get me to discuss when he could come back." She stopped again, lost in thought, then went on, "I think he was genuinely puzzled. He couldn't see how I felt."

She looked bleakly at Chris. "I hated him. I suppose it was sheer frustration on my part because I couldn't handle the situation. It was made worse because I had sat down with the children and explained that Daddy wasn't going to live with us any more. And there he was turning up all over the place! He'd call in after breakfast on Saturday or Sunday and suggest we all went out for the day!" Lyddy shook her head in memory of it. "Nikki and Peter didn't know what was going on. Looking back, I think they handled it all rather well."

She took another deep breath. This was quite difficult for her still. "Anyway, one evening he rang up and suggested going to the forest on the Saturday and I said why didn't he take the children and I would pack them a picnic." She glanced at Chris. "It was my way of getting everyone to adjust to the children seeing their father on their own without me. He argued but I made an excuse about having something to do that day. So on the Saturday morning, I made them up a picnic, got them ready to bundle out as soon as he arrived."

Lyddy moved over to the kitchen table and sat with her elbows resting on it, hands clasped in front of her. "He didn't turn up. He was supposed to come at ten. He was a real stickler for time, a stickler for everything. At half past, I phoned his flat, no answer. I kept ringing every so often. The children were getting fed up. I said he probably had to go into work early for a while, which he sometimes did on a Saturday. I even phoned his work, but he hadn't been seen and wasn't expected.

"By lunch time, I was getting really worried." She shot a glance at Chris, "I didn't love him any more, far from it, but it was so unlike him. He never altered plans without virtually having a board meeting and sending memos all round." She looked at her hands, still clasped in front of her. Chris moved across and sat in the chair opposite her.

"In the end, about two o'clock, I phoned Annie, my sister, and asked her to go round to his flat. I suppose I was afraid to go. I didn't want to show concern. Stupid, really. Anyway, I didn't want to take the children with me. So Annie went to the flat and came round to the house to say it was all locked up. The neighbours hadn't heard him about since the evening before. He had this awful habit of putting the news on the radio really loud so that he could hear it in all the rooms as he moved about. That was when I decided to phone the police to see if there had been any accidents or anything reported which might throw some light. I had to give details, description and all that."

Lyddy picked up her coffee cup to drink but saw it was empty and put it back on the table. Chris got up and switched the kettle on, making more coffee while Lyddy went on. "Two policemen turned up about half an hour later and asked to come in." She looked over at Chris as she spoke, "That was when I realised something was really wrong. It all became unreal then. I took them into the kitchen. Annie stayed with the children in the lounge. It turned out that the body of a man had been found by a dog walker in the woods, on the path leading from the park, the evening before, about eight o'clock. There had been a really bad storm, high winds. Apparently, a rotten branch had been blown down and struck this man while he was out, probably jogging – he had a track suit on. They described the track suit. It was the same as David's. He had no identification on him, only a door key on a chain round his neck, nothing in his pockets."

She brought her hands up and covered her face with them, speaking through the gap between them, immersed in the memory. "They took me to see the body. It was David. He had an enormous gash on the side of his head." Lyddy sat in silence, remembering her guilt and horror as she stood staring at David's still face. The blood had congealed in his hair above his right ear, thick, almost black.

She laid her arms back on the table and lifted her head to focus on Chris who had resumed her seat across from her. "So that was that. I'm afraid I went to pieces for a few days. Not hysterical or anything like that. Apart from the horror of it all I felt guilty because my overwhelming reaction was relief. It seemed wrong. Annie took the children home with her. I couldn't tell them straight away. She fended off the questions as well as she could." Lyddy gave a small smile, "You know how they ask questions. Annie offered to tell them for me but I wanted to. I just had to have time to gather myself together and take it all in.

"Will came over and stayed. We got terribly drunk, at least I did and I stayed drunk for about two days." She breathed in deeply. "Then I woke up, with the grandmother of hangovers, ready to face the world. And Annie brought the children back."

"How did they take it?" It was the first time Chris had spoken since Lyddy started her story.

"Very hard, initially. Lots of tears, questions, you know. But at their age, 'forever' is hard for them to contemplate. As it turned out, it took some time for it to really sink in with them. And because it took time, the blow wasn't as bad as I feared. They adjusted over a period. It was much easier for me than I had anticipated. I made an extra special effort to spend lots of time with them and to get on with life and they sort of took their cue from me.

"It was hard sometimes. Nikki used to sit and do pictures and paintings and write 'To Daddy, Love Nikki' on them with lots of kisses and she would ask whether he could see them in heaven."

Lyddy drank from her cup, leaning back in her chair. Chris contemplated all this while she watched Lyddy, then she stood up and walked round the table. She took Lyddy's hand, pulling her gently to her feet, and moved so that she was leaning against the kitchen worktop with her arms around her. Lyddy put her head on Chris's shoulder.

After a while, without moving, Chris murmured, "I'm so glad I met you."

Lyddy hugged her tightly, "So am I." She pulled her head back from Chris's shoulder to look into her face. "I'm alright," she said. "It brings it all back, talking about it. It's just draining." She gave a small grin, "Give us a kiss." They kissed, a long, deep kiss, pressing their bodies together, hands roaming inside their clothes.

Chris drew her head back first, "Oh, here we go again. I think I'd better go. I don't feel very strong willed at the moment."

Lyddy screwed her face up, "I wish you could stay."

Chris was thinking of the week ahead, "Can you get a baby-sitter next weekend? Friday or Saturday?"

"Friday. I'll arrange one for Friday."

They kissed again and just held each other for a long time.

"Will you be taking the children home tomorrow?" Lyddy asked eventually. Practical matters.

"Yes, of course. I'll see you after school. Well, briefly anyway."

They walked out of the kitchen arm-in-arm and Lyddy rested her head on Chris's shoulder, "Well, behave yourself when I come to pick them up," she said. "No snogging in the kitchen while they're outside in the garden."

Chris laughed. They stopped and wrapped their arms around each other again at the front door. "I'm really glad I came round," Chris said. Lyddy was too.

Chris opened the front door and left with a last kiss, "See you tomorrow, sweet dreams."

Chapter Nine

Lyddy didn't get to Chris's house the next afternoon. By then, she was at the hospital.

"Christ Almighty! Move over!" She cursed the driver in front. He had positioned himself in the middle of the left hand lane to turn right, instead of pulling over towards the centre of the road. She couldn't get by. She looked at her watch but didn't register the time.

"Head injury," the school secretary had said. "Unconscious." Those were the words that stuck in her mind.

The oncoming cars passed and the car in front turned off. Lyddy put her foot down, going through the gears. She tried to recall the rest of the conversation but she couldn't, only words. She drove through the traffic mechanically, overtaking, horns blaring at her.

She had just come down from her classroom for lunch when a boy had run up to her with a note: "Mrs Craven. Phone call. Urgent." The lady at reception sitting holding the phone out to her. The voice on the phone. The boiler room. Miss Carter. Ambulance. Oh, God, which hospital did she say? It must be this one.

She pulled into the main entrance, searching the signboards. Orthopaedics. Clementine Wing. Accident and Emergency. She followed the arrows and saw a large entrance, an ambulance pulling away. Nowhere to park. She looked up a side turning. "Disabled Parking Only." She turned the wheel and drove into one of the spaces. Grabbing her bag and the keys, she got out of the car and ran.

She pushed open the big main doors. Rows of seats, half filled, people waiting. Nurses milling to and fro. Desk. Reception. "Excuse me. My son has been brought here. Where...?"

The nurse behind the desk looked up. "What name?"

"Craven. Peter Craven."

"When was he brought here?"

"I don't know. Twenty minutes ago, maybe."

The nurse tapped buttons on the terminal keyboard in front of her and looked at the screen.

"Lyddy!"

Lyddy turned. Chris was coming towards her. She looked pale and worried. Lyddy fought back the tears and grabbed Chris's hand, "What happened? Where is he?"

"Mrs Craven!" The nurse was addressing her from behind. She turned back. "See that nurse over there, by the office. She will help you."

Lyddy strode across the wide corridor. "Excuse me! I'm looking for my son. Peter Craven. He was brought here about twenty minutes ago."

The nurse looked kindly at her. She put her hand on Lyddy's arm. "He's gone for X-ray and CT Scan," she said. "If you wait here, I'll let you know any news." She indicated the rows of chairs.

"CT Scan. What's a CT Scan?"

The nurse was patient, understanding. "He had a nasty knock on the head," she explained. "To check everything's alright."

The school secretary had said unconscious. "Has he come round? Is he conscious?"

The nurse looked sympathetically at Lyddy. "No, not yet."

"Oh, my God." Lyddy felt slightly sick.

"Wait over there," the nurse said, still kindly. "I'll let you know. Get yourself a cup of coffee." She gestured towards a drinks machine. Another nurse came up to her and she walked away, inclining her head as the other spoke.

Lyddy turned round. Chris was standing behind her, listening to the conversation. "Oh, Chris!" Lyddy controlled her panic.

Chris took her arm in hers and squeezed it. She led her to some chairs near the corner of a large alcove, "Come and sit down. I'll get us a coffee." She looked, concerned, at Lyddy, "You just have to wait. You know what these places are." She squeezed her arm again, "He's being looked after."

Lyddy sat down, fighting her impatience. Chris dug for change in her bag and got two cups of coffee out of the machine. She put the coffees on a table covered with magazines and sat next to Lyddy, taking her hand. Lyddy's dread showed in her face as she looked to Chris for answers, "What happened?" She shook her head a little, "I didn't catch it on the phone."

Chris kept hold of Lyddy's hand as she spoke, "It was an accident. It was the start of the lunch break. Apparently, he climbed onto the roof of the boiler room in the playground." Her face showed her vexation, that no one had seen him in time. It wasn't high, about five feet. The boiler room was in the basement, steps going down, but...

"What the hell... ? What was he doing up there?"

Chris shook her head, she couldn't answer that. "Anyway, his foot caught as he was about to jump down. He must have put his arm out to try to break his fall." She squeezed Lyddy's hand, "Lyddy, he broke his arm as well. Badly."

"How do you mean, badly?"

"The bone was showing through. I was in my classroom and saw the commotion. I ran over." She looked horrified.

"Oh, God!" Lyddy stared vacantly, not seeing the busy corridor, the people coming and going. She turned to Chris, "I'm so glad you went with him."

"Mrs Carlisle said someone should come to the hospital, until you could get here. I volunteered."

Lyddy was grateful. Chris went on, "Lyddy, I can't stay. I'll have to get back to school." The thought of leaving her here on her own was terrible. "I'll come back after school. Can I phone anyone for you?"

Lyddy brought her thoughts together. She would have to get on the phone. Nikki was still at school. Phone Annie. Should she phone her dad? She turned to Chris, "No, it's alright." She started looking in her purse. "Have you got any change?"

Chris gave her all the silver she'd got in her bag and quickly drank her coffee. "I feel awful leaving you."

"It's alright," Lyddy said again, wishing she didn't have to go. "I'll be alright. Could you see Nikki for me? Tell her not to worry. Tell her Annie will collect her from school. I'll try to see her later."

"Of course, I will."

They stood up and Chris put her arm through Lyddy's again as they walked to the main entrance and through the big doors.

"How will you get back to school?" Lyddy asked.

"I've got my car. I followed the ambulance." Her concern showed on her face. "I hate leaving you. Phone me if you need to. The school won't mind."

"Okay." Lyddy put on a grim smile and they hugged each other for several seconds. Lyddy fought back the tears again as she watched Chris walk off around the corner.

Lyddy went back to where she had been sitting. She saw the nurse she had spoken to and caught her attention. She came over shaking her head, sympathetically again. "They haven't brought him back yet. I'll let you know. Try not to worry." She walked away, busy.

Lyddy sat down again, her thoughts falling over one another. She thought of David's still body, the matted blood around his wound. She pushed the image away. She wondered vaguely which arm was broken; Peter was right handed. Her thoughts tumbled over each other and went away. She sat there numbly, blank, her tension and anxiety taking over.

She became aware of the nurse coming towards her, a smile across her face. "They've brought him back," she said. "I think they're going to see to his arm now. The doctor will come and see you in a minute. I just had a word with him. He knows you're here." She added, kindly, "Have you had a cup of coffee?" There was little else she could offer.

"Yes, thank you."

The nurse went away again.

Lyddy had a target for her attention now. She sat watching as patients, nurses, the occasional doctor came and went through the part of the corridor she could see. A man on a stretcher was wheeled through, the three paramedics almost on the run, one of them holding something on the man's stomach. A little girl limped past with her mum.

A doctor walked past, put his head round the office door and then turned to look over to where Lyddy was sitting. He came over to her. Lyddy stood up, searching his face for a clue.

"Mrs Craven?"

"Yes." Lyddy waited, almost holding her breath, feeling only terror. The doctor sat down next to Lyddy's chair and Lyddy sat too, turned towards him.

"Right. Peter. He's had a very bad knock on the head. He's been for a scan," he allowed himself a small, reassuring smile. "There's no apparent damage done. We have to check in these cases that there is no blood clot or swelling of the blood vessels. The X-ray showed that there is no fracture of the skull. He's conscious now," he added.

Lyddy raised her eyebrows, waiting for him to continue. He did.

"He has suffered severe concussion. The fact that he's conscious now is obviously a good sign. There will be further tests we will have to do. They'll do those when he is moved to a ward. We have to set his arm now. He has a compound fracture of the left forearm." He looked at Lyddy to see if he should explain. Lyddy nodded, she understood, so he went on. "He will have to be anaesthetised; it's a nasty break. It has to be realigned and the damaged tissue sewn up. He'll have a cast on. I understand he hadn't had lunch when this happened?"

"No." Peter was in the second dinners sitting. "Can I see him?"

The doctor shook his head, "No, not yet. They're just getting him ready." He stood up. "He'll be taken to a ward afterwards. The nurse will let you know." He indicated the office and glanced at Lyddy to see if that was sufficient for her, "Okay?"

"Yes, thank you."

The doctor hurried away. It was a routine, busy day for him.

Lyddy took a deep breath, expelling it slowly as she took in what the doctor had told her. She wished she could see Peter, just for a minute. She resigned herself to patience. A fleeting thought crossed her mind of how she would have been feeling now had the doctor's news been different. The frailty of life. She mentally shook her head to clear the thought. Just be grateful.

She stood up, taking her purse out of her bag, looking around for phones. Who first? she wondered. Annie, then Dad, she decided, and Peter's school, let them know; Nikki and Chris too. She would phone her own school later, she would need a day or two off.

Lyddy sat on a chair pushed up close to the bed. She held Peter's hand in her own. He had come round briefly from the anaesthetic and nodded off again. His left arm was in a cast from just above his elbow to his hand, the tips of his fingers poking out. A drip line was inserted into his right hand, the point of entry patched over with white elastoplast. A urine bag hung at the side of the bed leading from the catheter. He had a dressing on his forehead, just at the hairline. His pale face composed in sleep, he murmured from time to time.

Lyddy was grateful that she had a focus now, to be here with him. He was in a small room on the ward, on his own, near the nurses' station. He would probably be moved to another room tomorrow with other beds. She had asked the doctor how long he was likely to be kept in. He told her that they would do further tests in the morning, but he would have to stay for at least a couple of days. Apart from anything else, it would take a day or two for the effects of the concussion to wear off. He would be very sleepy and have a tendency to vomit. The doctor had intimated that they err on the side of caution with head injuries. He wouldn't be allowed home until they were completely satisfied that all was well.

The afternoon had seemed interminable to Lyddy. She had made her phone calls. Her dad insisted on coming down. She had tried to dissuade him and then thought, why not? Of course he wants to come. She hadn't been able to get hold of Annie so she'd left a message on the answer phone and then phoned Bob at work. Annie was at the 'club'. He promised to get hold of her and pass the message on to collect Nikki from school. He offered to come to the hospital but she said no, there was nothing to do here. She was alright.

She had even thought to phone Mr Burberry. He was keeping Dodger with him tonight. He was pleased to be able to help.

Finally, at last, the nurse had come over to see her. She told her which ward Peter had been taken to and gave her directions. It had still been another half an hour before they had let her into the room.

Lyddy sat there now, aware of the hospital noises outside the room: phone ringing, nurses voices, laughter, the rattling of a tea trolley. She didn't know how long she had sat there. She glanced at her watch. It was five o'clock. Less than five hours since the phone call. It seemed forever. The worry, tension and suspense had worn her out, leaving her empty inside. She watched Peter's face, aware of how vulnerable you are when you have children; how devastating it is when something befalls them, worse than if it happens to yourself. The relief was beginning to push its way through the stress of the afternoon.

The door into the room opened and a nurse came in, holding a metal tray with bottles, syringes, dressings on it. "I'm just going to see to him now," she said. "Give him a painkiller and so on. Why don't you go and get something to eat?" They were all so cheerful but sympathetic at the same time. Lyddy looked questioningly at her.

"You can come back later," she said. "He won't wake up much before the morning, but you'll be able to come and sit with him again. Go and get some tea," she urged, dismissing Lyddy in a kindly way.

Lyddy looked back at Peter, still holding his hand, reluctant to release the contact. She stood up and walked out of the room, suddenly feeling the fatigue from the horror of it all. It hit her now that he was going to be alright, that her worst fears had come to nothing.

As she closed the door behind her, she saw Chris coming across the corridor. She must have been waiting. Her face showed her concern for what Lyddy had been through. At the sight of her, Lyddy felt the tears coming again and tried to force them back, but the tension was gone now and she couldn't control them. They came as Chris held her arms out to hug her. She slid her arms inside Chris's open coat and hugged her waist, pressing her face into Chris's neck, aware of crying in a public place. Chris slipped the fingers of one hand through Lyddy's hair at the back of her head and held her cheek to Lyddy's. They stood there, Lyddy letting it all go and Chris saying nothing, just holding her tightly.

After a while, Lyddy's sobs lessened and she said into Chris's neck, "He's alright. He's going to be okay."

"I know." Chris had got the message at school. She tightened her arm around Lyddy's waist and pressed her lips to her cheek for several moments.

When she felt in control again, Lyddy raised her head. The tears had smudged her make-up which she wore for school. Her cheeks were wet. Chris smiled at her, glad she had found the release. "Do you want a tissue?" She dug in her pockets.

Lyddy started blowing her nose and wiping her cheeks and suddenly spied her father and Annie standing side by side a few steps away, unwilling to intrude.

Annie's face echoed her confusion and amazement at the sight of Peter's teacher wrapped around Lyddy in a manner one could only describe as intimate. Despite herself, Lyddy smiled inwardly. She forgot sometimes how astute Annie could be.

Her pent-up emotions now back on the level, Lyddy couldn't help herself. She grinned, "Annie, your mouth's open."

Annie shut it quickly and composed her face. She came forward, glancing at Chris before taking Lyddy's shoulders in both hands. "Oh, Lyddy!" Annie hugged her and held her at arm's length. "I couldn't believe it when Bob phoned. How is he? You just don't know what's going to happen next, do you? I phoned the hospital to make sure Peter was alright. The nurse wouldn't tell me straight away. She asked if I was a relative. 'Of course I'm a relative, I'm his Aunt,' I said. Even then, she would only give me the bare bones. But," she paused for breath, "Oh, Lyddy," she said again, "at least he's going to be alright. Have you been here all on your own? I was going to come over but Bob said not to. I wouldn't have had time if I was to collect Nikki. She's at home, by the way. Bob came home early. He was playing cricket in the garden with her when we left. Oh, I just can't help thinking how it might have turned out. You must have been out of your mind. Dad's here, look, he's staying with us. I suppose they'll keep him in for a while. Poor darling."

Annie ran out of steam. Before she could regenerate, Lyddy gently prised herself out of Annie's grasp to turn to her father. He was waiting patiently, watching the scene, a small smile on his face.

"Hello, Dad. Thanks for coming."

"Hello, darling. Is he okay?"

"Yes, he will be."

They hugged each other in silence, then stood back, holding hands. At seventy-five, her father was looking healthy and fit. His hair was almost white now but it looked good on him. "Are you alright, my love?"

"Yes, I'm fine. Peter's sleeping." She made a face, indicating how awful it had been. He squeezed her hands in reply.

She turned and took a step to Chris's side, touching her elbow. "Chris, this is my father. Dad, this is Chris, Peter's teacher, and a friend," she added.

"Pleased to meet you." Her father held out his hand. Chris took it, returning his smile.

"This is Annie, my sister," Lyddy went on, turning back to Annie.

"Hello, I've seen you at school sometimes," Chris said, holding out her hand.

Annie took her fingers lightly and then let them go, for once searching for something to say. She forced a small smile. "I hear you came to the hospital with Peter." She glanced at Lyddy and back. "We're all very grateful."

Chris said simply, "I was glad to."

Lyddy's father quietly took charge. He held his arms out, steering them all towards the exit at the end of the corridor. "Come on, let's find the canteen. Lyddy, you must be starving and I'm gasping for a cuppa."

Much later, Lyddy sat at her kitchen table, her coffee cup empty, too exhausted to move. She looked at the clock, ten thirty. They hadn't allowed her to stay at the hospital. The rooms they used to keep for parents had been knocked into one to extend one of the departments. She hadn't liked leaving Peter but hadn't had a choice.

Her father and Annie had stayed for an hour or so while they had tea and chatted. For once, Annie was quiet – watchful, Lyddy thought. She smiled to herself. Annie would choose her moment.

The nurses hadn't let anyone else in to see Peter, much to Annie's chagrin, and she and her dad had left. Annie wanted to be home to put Nikki to bed. She was going to call into Lyddy's house to collect Nikki's things; Nikki would stay at Annie's tonight. Lyddy told her to give Nikki a kiss for her and to tell her that she would try to call in to see her before school in the morning.

Chris had stayed at the hospital with her, for which Lyddy was grateful. They both went back in to sit with Peter. He woke once and gave a little smile when he saw Lyddy. "Hello, Mum," he said sleepily.

"Hello, my darling."

He said his head hurt a bit but otherwise he couldn't feel anything. Lyddy called the nurse when he said he felt sick and they stood back while the nurse saw to him. When he had recovered, Lyddy sat down by him again. She told him she couldn't stay but would be back again in the morning.

"Okay, Mum." His eyes started closing again, "I love you."

She had gone back in again, briefly. He was still sleeping.

Finally the night nurse had shooed them out, telling her to get some sleep. Lyddy asked Chris if she would come back with her and stay.

"I was going to offer if you hadn't asked."

Chris came into the kitchen now and bent over the table, her forearms resting on it. "Come on, you look done in. You need a good night's sleep."

"I can't. I'm too tired."

Chris straightened up and pulled Lyddy to her feet. "Don't be belligerent. Go to bed. I'll switch the lights off and all that. Go." She pushed her towards the door.

Later, they lay in bed, talking quietly, arms around each other and legs entwined, that comfortable time before sleep. "I wish the circumstances had been different, but I'm so glad you're here," Lyddy murmured.

Chris ran her hand slowly down Lyddy's back, over her bottom and along her upper leg. She said, "Annie's guessed, hasn't she?"

"She's got a good idea; she just can't believe it. Don't worry, I can handle Annie. My Dad's guessed too."

"Has he? I like your dad. He's got a quiet strength."

"He liked you, too. I could tell."

Chris was thinking of Annie's open mouth, "Do you always take the mickey out of Annie?"

"As often as I can. Actually," Lyddy moved her head to get more comfortable, burying it in Chris's shoulder, kissing her neck, "believe it or not, we're very close. We're just very different."

They chatted on for a while and then fell asleep, Lyddy falling into a deep, dreamless sleep, recuperating after her wearying day.

Chapter Ten

They were ready to go at seven thirty the next morning. Lyddy phoned the ward at seven. Peter was fine. He was awake and waiting for his breakfast. She decided she would spend a bit of time with Nikki over at Annie's before going to the hospital. Chris had to go home for a change of clothes before school.

Lyddy stopped at the front door before opening it. "Will you stay again tonight?" Nikki would be staying at Annie's again.

"Yes, I will. Shall I come to the hospital?"

Lyddy thought Chris had done enough. "No, no need. I'll stay for the day and Nikki will want to see him, Annie and my dad, too. Peter's going to be tired by then. I won't stay so late tonight. Shall I see you here?" She fiddled with her key ring. "Have the back door key. You can let yourself in."

"What time?" Chris took the key.

"About seven? I'll do us something to eat."

They hugged for several moments.

"Thanks for yesterday," Lyddy said, "at the hospital."

"You don't need to thank me." Chris kissed her.

Lyddy grinned. "I've got to face Annie now."

"Does it worry you?"

"No, funnily enough." Lyddy looked at Chris, a determined look. "If she starts asking questions, I'm not going to lie to her."

"Good," Chris agreed with her and they hugged again. "I'll see you later."

Lyddy opened the front door and they each got into their cars and drove off out of the driveway.

Lyddy thought about Peter as she drove to Annie's, wondering how he would feel today, how he had spent the night, what tests they still had to do on him. She thought of his pale face on the pillow the night before, feeling relief again that her worst fears had not been realised.

Bob opened the door to her knock. He was dressed in an expensive dark suit and had his overcoat over his arm. A handsome man, greying, ageing with the grace that some men can. He was just leaving for work. He hugged Lyddy as she stepped into the house, "Lyddy. How are you? How's Peter?"

"He was fine when I left him last night. Just sleeping it all off."

"He was lucky, wasn't he?" Bob glanced at his watch. "I'm afraid I've got to go. I've got a breakfast meeting. Annie's in the kitchen." He kissed her on the cheek and passed through the still open doorway. "I'll see you soon. Give Peter my love."

"Bye, Bob. See you soon." Lyddy started to walk across the large square hall. The elegant stairway came down into the middle of it, well lit from a large, decorative casement window in the roof at the top of the stairwell.

Nikki appeared at the bend in the stairs, still in her pyjamas. "Mum!" She flew down the stairs and leapt the last three steps into Lyddy's arms, nearly knocking her off her feet.

" Hello, my darling. Goodness, you'll squeeze me to death. Have you been good?" Lyddy kissed her.

"Of course I have. Uncle Bob and I made a tent in the lounge and we had tea in there."

"I bet Annie was pleased. Let's go and see her." Lyddy carried Nikki through to the kitchen at the back of the house.

Annie looked up from the breakfast room set off from the kitchen, she was laying the table. "Hello, darling," she came over to kiss Lyddy. "Have you had breakfast?"

Lyddy said she would just have coffee. She hung her coat over the back of a chair. Annie picked the coat up and went to hang it on a peg in the small corridor leading from the kitchen. "Sit down. There's a pot of coffee made – help yourself." She came back into the kitchen, "Nikki, sit down sweetheart. Your breakfast's ready."

Nikki sat at the table and tucked into the plateful of bacon, egg and sausage which Annie put in front of her. "Mm, yum. At home, we only have cereal and toast for breakfast on school days."

"Yes, and see how well you look on it," said Lyddy, not to be drawn into that.

"Mum?" said Nikki, through her mouthful. She saw Lyddy's look and hurried to swallow before she went on. Lyddy waited. "Can I go and see Peter after school today?"

"Probably, darling. I'll see how he is today. Remember he will probably be a bit weary. I don't expect he'll get up much today."

"What! Stay in bed all day? How boring."

"Not if you don't feel well. I've got some things for him to do, in the car." She had brought some games and a couple of books. "Maybe Annie will bring you over after school." She looked questioningly at Annie.

"Yes of course, sweetheart. I'll pick you up from school and we'll go straight to the hospital. I expect Grandad will want to come as well."

"Where is Dad?" Lyddy asked. "Is he still in bed?"

"Lazy thing." Nikki put half a sausage in her mouth, her cheeks bulging as she chewed.

"Nikki, this isn't a race, you know." Annie was sitting now, holding her cup in both hands, leaning on her elbows.

"Mm, but it's nicer if you stuff a lot in."

Lyddy avoided Annie's where-does-she-get-her-table-manners look and said to Nikki, "You're going to stay here at Annie's again tonight. Is that alright?"

"Ooh, yes, lovely! Can we make the tent again, Aunty Annie?"

Nikki finished her breakfast and sat on Lyddy's lap for a cuddle while she drank her milk, telling her of the excitement when the ambulance came. "He looked awful, Mum. I cried 'cos I thought he was dead. But the dinner lady told me he wasn't dead and she made me go in to dinner. We heard the siren when the ambulance arrived and everyone rushed to the windows to look." She finished her milk.

Annie said, "Go upstairs and wash your face and hands now. Your uniform is on the chair by your bed. Don't forget to brush your teeth," she called out as Nikki ran out of the room.

Lyddy and Annie sat in silence, drinking their coffee. Lyddy didn't say anything. She didn't want to open a topic of conversation. She wanted Annie to get it off her chest.

"Lyddy." Annie was looking uncomfortable.

Lyddy waited.

"Peter's teacher."

"Chris."

"Chris. Yes." Annie was not often at a loss for words. "How well do you know her?" Annie forced herself to look at Lyddy.

"Very well."

Annie had to know. "Do you...? What kind of..." She started again, "Are you...?" She couldn't bring herself to finish the question.

Lyddy suppressed a grin and put her out of her misery. "Having an affair?" she finished it for her.

"Oh, Lord!" Annie put her cup down, her agitation too much for her.

Lyddy decided enough was enough, poor Annie. "Yes, we are."

Annie looked at her, her features stricken, frozen in disbelief. "An affair. You're having an affair. With a woman." She wasn't asking, she was stating, trying to impress it on her mind.

"Yes."

"Oh, my God," Annie breathed the words. She picked up her cup, didn't trust her grip and put it down. She collected herself and looked at Lyddy again. "I couldn't believe my eyes in the hospital. But then the way you looked at her sometimes, and she looked at you. In the canteen, I mean. I thought, they must be. Then I thought, no, they can't be." Her indignation came through. "How *could* you? With a *woman?*"

"I like her, Annie. I like her a lot. We laugh at the same things. I'm very attracted to her."

"Yes, but... Do you love her? You can't love her?" Annie was trying to understand.

Lyddy thought for a moment. It had all happened so quickly, her and Chris. But she knew this wasn't a casual affair. She wasn't going to feel any differently next week or next month. "It's very early days, Annie." She paused. In for a penny, she thought. "I know I haven't felt like this about anybody for a long time."

"Oh, my God." Annie murmured the words again. She was thinking furiously. "What will people say? What will Dad say?"

"Dad won't say anything. He knows anyway."

Annie's expression acknowledged the truth in Lyddy's words. "Yes, I asked him what he thought, on the way home from the hospital last night. All he would say was that he liked Chris and he just wanted you to be happy."

Lyddy silently blessed her father.

Annie went on, dismissing his reaction as unhelpful, "Yes, but what will other people say?"

"Annie, we're not going to put a notice in the local paper. We're not going to hold naked orgies in the front garden. We might have the odd one in the back." Annie looked up sharply. "I'm kidding, Annie. And anyway," Lyddy continued, remembering what she had said to Chris, "I'm thirty-seven. I don't think what other people say matters too much. If they're friends they will understand. If they're not, well, they can mind their own business." Lyddy found herself believing her own words. Talking about it was driving away any disquiet she had in her own mind.

Annie tried once more, "But what about the children? What will they think?"

"They like Chris. She talks to them and she makes them laugh. And we're not going to gather them together and make an announcement." She felt she should calm Annie's fears on this score. She wasn't mocking now. "Annie, we'll be discreet. They'll get used to Chris being around. They'll have time to adjust. Don't worry about them."

Lyddy looked at Annie's face and decided to go easy on her. "Annie, I can't analyse it for you. It just is." But she added, to help Annie understand, "It took me by surprise too, you know."

Annie gave up. Lyddy obviously had faith in her own conviction. "Is this going to last?" she asked.

Lyddy thought again. "Yes," she said. "I think it is."

"Okay." Annie had taken in enough for the moment. She would need to think it all over. Lyddy was her sister. She didn't understand her sometimes, but she loved her. She would have to try to adjust to this. She would talk to Bob, tonight. She stood up. "I'd better get Nikki to school. Are you off soon?"

Lyddy stood up as well. "Yes, I'll get going. I'll see Nikki first."

Annie came round the table and hugged Lyddy lightly, "I want you to be happy as well." She looked Lyddy in the face. "I'll do my best," she said. "Try to adjust, accept."

"I know you will," Lyddy answered. She grinned, "It's not the end of the world."

"I'm sure it's not," Annie said without conviction, then added, "Nor was Hiroshima, dear." She caught Lyddy's look and allowed herself the trace of a smile, "Well! You know what I mean. That caused quite a commotion for the people concerned, didn't it?"

"Oh, Annie!"

"Anyway, it's time to go." Annie gathered herself and went to the door to call Nikki down.

Lyddy got her coat and went through to the hall as Nikki came downstairs. She bent down to do Nikki's shoelaces up for her and gave her a hug and a kiss. Nikki put her coat on as she followed Lyddy outside to where her car was parked on the wide, sweeping driveway.

"Bye, sweetheart," Lyddy bent to give her another kiss. "I love you. I'll see you at the hospital this afternoon."

"Bye, Mum. Love you." Nikki waved as Lyddy drove off and she ran back to where Annie was watching from the doorway.

Chapter Eleven

Lyddy held the new door handle against the door and marked inside the holes where the screws would go. It was the door leading from the kitchen to the utility room and the catch kept sticking. She reached for the drill and drilled short holes at each mark to start off the screws. The sound of the drill drowned the hubbub of noise from the children at the table.

"Mu-um!" Nikki and Peter called out, exasperated as she started and stopped the drill each time.

"Alright. I've nearly finished."

They were sitting with Jane's three children, playing Ludo. Jane and her husband had gone to a wedding so Lyddy had invited them round for the afternoon. It was company for Peter. He had been allowed home the day before, and Lyddy had been told he should take it easy for a day or two. The doctor said he could go back to school on Monday but no running around the playground for a while.

"Oh, Tom! You've landed on me again! You're doing it on purpose. You could have moved that one and sent Peter back home!"

"I can move which one I like."

"Yes, but I've only got two out now!"

"Alice, put it back. It's been sent home. You have to put it back." Paul, the eldest of them all at eleven, was referee, to stem the inevitable disagreements.

Lyddy let the voices go over her head. She was enjoying a Saturday at home, catching up on a string of jobs.

Her father had called in an hour before, to say good-bye; he had been at Annie's since Monday and was ready to go home. The children were upstairs then, so she sat with him at the kitchen table. He asked her what plans she had for the coming Easter.

"I haven't really thought about it yet."

"Why don't you bring the children up to stay over the long weekend?"

"Isn't that a bit too much for you?"

"No, of course not. I'm not in the last stages of decay yet. I'll let you help with the cooking if it makes you feel better."

"The children would love it." Her dad's house was close to the Thames. He lived in a village some miles up its route from Oxford, not even a village, more a collection of houses and a pub. Nikki and Peter loved messing about by the river.

"Maybe Chris would like to come, too."

Lyddy smiled her appreciation, "Thank you, Dad. I'll ask her."

It struck Lyddy where she got her sense of humour from when he said, "I'm afraid you'll have to share a room, though. I'm not having guests sleeping on the sofa. I hope that won't be a problem," his face deadpan.

"We'll manage," Lyddy said, meeting his eye. Then she grinned happily, "Really, Dad, Annie would throw a fit if she heard you."

"Oh, Annie doesn't frighten me. Anyway, you can get away with more as you get older. People just think you're losing your marbles."

Lyddy smiled. Then she couldn't help asking, "Were you shocked?"

"No, darling. Surprised, not shocked." He laughed, "Annie, now, you sent Annie into a panic, to say the least."

"I know." Lyddy paused. "I didn't intend all this fuss, you know. It's just the way it worked out."

He shrugged, unperturbed. "I know you didn't. It's probably better, all out in the open." Then he added, as an afterthought, "I like Chris very much. You suit each other." And he smirked, about to make fun of her, "I hope you'll be very happy together."

Lyddy affected a grave demeanour, "Thank you, Father. I hope so too."

He had left after saying good-bye to the children, declining the offer of a meal. He wanted to get home in daylight.

Lyddy placed one of the door handles against the door and pushed each screw in as far as it would go. She started screwing them home. It had been quite a week, she thought, starting with that awful day on Monday. The school had been good and allowed her two days compassionate leave. Peter seemed quite himself by Wednesday, except for his arm of course. But they weren't taking any chances. They insisted on keeping him in for another forty-eight hours. Lyddy had gone to the hospital after school on Friday to bring him home.

Chris had gone for her job interview on Thursday. Four candidates were interviewed. They were asked to wait for all the interviews to be over and for the panel to make its decision. They offered Chris the job. Lyddy was pleased for her; she deserved it. She was putting aside thoughts of what it would mean. September was a long way off.

Chris had come round when she got back on Thursday evening, after Nikki had gone to bed. Lyddy opened the door to her and stood facing her at the open doorway, waiting for her news.

Chris stood still on the doorstep, her features impassive. "I got it."

Lyddy wanted to make sure, "And you accepted?"

"Yes, I did." Chris smiled but her pleasure didn't quite show in her eyes as it usually did.

Lyddy felt sorry that what should have been cause for celebration was marred by the obvious implication. She roused herself to make better of it for Chris. She put out her hand to lead her in through the doorway. "Well done! I knew you would." She hugged Chris and almost shook her by the shoulders. "You must be pleased? Don't worry about what will happen. Your job's important, isn't it?"

"Yes, I know." She took a deep breath, "Oh, Lyddy. I know it's a long way off and I know we haven't known each other very long and I know I'm being stupid but, well, September will come rushing round and before you know it..." She didn't finish. They would be living eighty miles apart.

Lyddy reflected again how honest and open Chris was, even with herself. Cards on the table, nothing hidden.

Lyddy had kept up her resolve; she wasn't going to weaken. "It'll work out," she told her in a confident tone. She searched for something cheerful to say, "And it is nearly five months away." She hugged Chris again, saying, "You're brilliant. Well done." She kissed her lips and took her arm. "Come on, I got a bottle of champagne on the way back from the hospital. To celebrate."

"You obviously have faith in me."

Lyddy didn't say that they could have celebrated either way. Instead she had said, "I knew you'd get the job."

Now she picked up the second door handle, to put on the other side. Kneeling, she held it against the door, aligning it with the screw holes and she reached for the screws. There was a knock on the back door.

"Come in!" Nikki and Peter called from the table.

It was Chris. Lyddy had asked her round to have a meal with them. She wanted her there while the children were up. Lyddy sat back on her heels and watched as she came into the room, feeling sheer delight at the sight of her.

"Hi, everyone!"

She was looking cheerful, Lyddy thought, glad she had stuck to her guns to convince her that all would be well.

Chris bent down over Peter's shoulder to speak, "Hi, Peter. How's your arm?"

The dressing was off his head now, the bruise yellowing. "It's alright. It hurts a bit, sometimes." He showed her the cast, already covered in names and drawings.

She straightened up and looked round the table, "Who's winning?"

"Me," said Nikki and Tom together. Tom was Jane's youngest, the same age as Nikki. They started arguing about who was closest to winning with the most counters.

Chris walked over to where Lyddy was kneeling. They smiled at each other and Chris put her hand on Lyddy's shoulder. "Hello."

"Hello." Lyddy covered Chris's hand with her own and met her eyes for a few moments. How long was it since she had been attracted to someone like this? She couldn't even remember. She could feel her insides warming up and loved the feeling. She glanced at her handiwork. "Running repairs. I'm getting a bit of a dab-hand. I've fixed Peter's toy box, put new sealant round the bath, glued two toys back together and put new door handles on. Well, nearly. I've nearly finished."

"Can I do anything?"

"Not really. The casserole's in the oven. You can put the kettle on. I'll just put this lot away and we'll take a cup of tea in the sitting room. It's quiet in there." Lyddy grinned at the rabble of voices and raised her own voice, "Anyone want a drink?"

There was a chorus of replies. Chris said, "I'll get them. You finish that."

Ten minutes later, Chris led the way into the sitting room. She put the tea down on the small table and turned back to Lyddy, coming in behind her. She put her arms around Lyddy and pushed her back towards the door, reaching out a hand to push it shut. She pressed herself against her, Lyddy's back to the door.

Lyddy was smiling. "I told Annie we would be discreet," she said, making no effort to resist.

"They won't come bursting in. Not straight away, anyway." Chris put her face up close to Lyddy's. "I couldn't wait. Till the children go to bed." She pressed her mouth onto Lyddy's, working her way in, finding her tongue.

Lyddy wrapped her arms round Chris and squeezed her body more tightly to hers, lost in the kiss. When it finished, she opened her mouth on to Chris's again for more.

"That feels lovely. I've missed you," Chris breathed, running her lips over Lyddy's mouth.

"Good. I'm glad," Lyddy laughed softly. "It's been all of two days."

"Shall we have our tea now?" Chris nuzzled her face into Lyddy's neck. "You'd better open the door. Dodger will get suspicious."

Chris got her cup of tea and sat in one of the easy chairs. Lyddy settled back on the arm of it with her arm around Chris's shoulder.

"We've been invited to Will's next Saturday. Are you doing anything?"

"We?"

"Yes, he knows about you." Lyddy swallowed a sly grin. "He phoned last night to ask us over."

"No, I've nothing planned. Well, there was a message on the answer phone when I got in this afternoon. An invite to some friends, next Saturday. I haven't called them back yet." Chris looked up at Lyddy and added, a little drolly, "I don't think I could have asked to take you to Anne and Simon's. Not yet anyway." She raised her eyebrows.

Lyddy didn't dwell on it. "We'll make a good foursome at Will's."

"Why?"

"He lives with his boyfriend, Carl."

"Oh, I see."

"You'll love him, I hope, and Carl too. Carl's lovely. He tells awful jokes, though."

It appealed to Chris and she smiled, "So do I. I look forward to it."

They sat for a while, drinking their tea and talking. A car pulled into the drive.

Lyddy kissed the top of Chris's head and got up. "There's Jane to collect her brood. When they've gone I'll organise the kitchen and we can eat." She went to the front door as the bell rang.

Jane stood on the doorstep looking immaculately dishevelled, clutching her hat in her hand, eyes bloodshot. "I seem to be a bit the worse for wear." Her words ran into each other and she giggled.

Lyddy laughed and stepped aside for her to come in, "Good wedding, I take it." She looked out of the doorway. Jane's husband had stayed at the wheel, staring ahead of him. "Jack not coming in?"

Jane let out a staccato laugh, "No, he's gone into 'disgusted' mode." She stepped heavily off the doormat, misjudging its depth, "Whoops! He's been moaning at me all the way back." She put on a heavy tone, "Why do you have to *drink* so much at these events! I suppose you'll *collapse* when we get home and *I'll* have to see to the children." She laughed again, "That'll make a change."

She started towards the kitchen and stopped as she caught sight of Chris through the open sitting room door, "Oh, God, how embarrassing." She looked back at Lyddy, "Why didn't you tell me!" She had only met Chris before at the school.

"Hi, there," Chris's grin widened at the sight of her. "You look as though you've had a good time."

Jane clapped her hat on her head at an angle and started laughing, leaning in the doorway, "I really am a very responsible mother, normally. Ask anyone. Ask Jack!" She slumped a bit and giggled, "Don't ask him at the moment, though."

Lyddy laughed and took her elbow, "Come and get your offspring, otherwise you won't make it home before you collapse."

Jane let herself be led down the hall and hiccuped, "What is it about weddings?"

"It's the champagne," Lyddy told her. "I remember Jack telling you to lay off the champagne at a party once."

"Did he?"

"Yes. You didn't take any notice of him then, either."

Amidst giggles from Jane every time she hiccuped, Lyddy herded them all out to the car. Jack sat there tight-lipped as Jane fell heavily into the passenger seat. "What's for dinner, darling?" she asked, going off into paroxysms of laughter. Jack managed a polite nod at Lyddy before he drove off.

Lyddy was smiling as she went back into the sitting room. "She'll have an almighty hangover tomorrow, and be vowing never to touch another drop ever again. I know that feeling all too well."

Chris laughed and Lyddy bent to pick up the mugs, stopping to run her hand through Chris's hair, "We can go and eat now."

They sat round the table with Nikki and Peter. That pleasant time, after eating and before the children disappeared to play and the clearing up had to be done. Lyddy was leaning back in her chair, listening to the conversation, feeling happy with her lot.

They were talking dogs. Dodger had appeared from the garden that morning carrying a mouse. "He dropped it on the floor under the table and started pushing it with his nose," Peter was telling Chris. "I think he wanted to play with it."

"Silly Dodger, it was already dead," Nikki joined in. "Poor thing, we buried it in the garden. Mummy made a cross out of lollipop sticks. Do mice go to heaven, Mum?"

"I don't know, sweetheart. Probably."

Peter looked at Chris. "Our daddy's in heaven."

"Yes, I know."

"Do you like dogs, Chris?" It was Nikki's question. "You must do, 'cos Dodger likes you. Dogs can tell, can't they?"

Chris told them about her dog when she was younger. She wrinkled her nose, "There was just one thing wrong with her. She had this awful habit of cleaning up after other dogs, eating things she shouldn't eat."

"What, like dead rats and things?" Nikki was impressed.

"Well, no, other dogs'..." Chris searched for a suitable word.

"Poo!" Nikki and Peter said together.

Nikki couldn't let this rest. "She eated other dogs' poo? Oh, yuk!"

Peter wasn't so shocked. He said to Nikki, "Don't you remember? Mrs Peterson's dog used to do that. What was her name, Mum?"

"Candy."

Peter turned to Chris. "She used to do a poo out in the garden and then go back later and gobble it up."

Lyddy intervened, "Oh, my Lord. What a charming after-dinner conversation. Can't you do better than that?" They all laughed.

Peter wasn't put off. "Grandad told me that Aunty Annie ate her own poo when she was little. She took it out of her potty." Lyddy smiled; this story had been told before. Peter went on, telling Chris. "I asked her once if she remembered doing it and she said," he put on his best Aunty Annie voice, "'I did no such thing. Really! Your grandad makes these stories up.'" He continued in his own voice, "But Grandad said she did really." Peter's face was a picture.

Lyddy shook her head, amused, mostly at the children's delight in the story. Poor Annie. She stood up. "If that's the best you can do, I think it's time we washed up. Go on, you two, skedaddle."

They cleared up from the meal; Lyddy bathed Nikki and Peter, and Chris read them a story, at Nikki's request. She read a Worzel Gummidge story, mimicking Worzel's accent to a tee. They said she was nearly as good as their mum. Chris went downstairs while Lyddy got them into bed.

Lyddy came down into the kitchen and unburdened herself of an armful of dirty washing on to the kitchen top. She went over to where Chris was sitting at the table, reading the paper. Bending, she put her arms round Chris's neck from behind and rested her cheek against hers. "I like your Worzel accent."

Chris put the voice on now, "Well, it comes from havin' a lot of practise."

"I love having you here." Lyddy rubbed her cheek against Chris's and moved her mouth down to her neck. "I could eat you, bit by bit."

Chris pulled Lyddy's arms down over her chest and covered them with her own. She leant back in her chair and Lyddy kissed her from above.

"What would you like to do?" Lyddy asked. They were staying in; she didn't want to leave Peter with a baby-sitter.

"I'd like to loll on the sofa. With you and a drink handy." Chris stretched her neck to kiss Lyddy again.

"Right. That's what we'll do. I'll put my new CD on."

They lay on the sofa, Tanita Tikaram playing on the stereo, gin and tonics within reach on the floor. Lyddy had switched the fire on and Dodger sprawled contentedly in front of it.

They talked about what they were doing the next day, Sunday. Chris was having lunch with friends and Lyddy was taking the children to the cinema. She didn't want to do anything too energetic with Peter.

"By the way," Lyddy said, pushing herself up to rest on her elbow, "Are you doing anything over Easter?"

Chris said she was staying at a friend's for a couple of days during the week before and would stop at her parents, for a night or two on the way back.

"Well, you're invited to my dad's with us for the Easter weekend."

"Really?"

"Yes, you've obviously made a good impression."

"He's lovely. I like your dad."

"Well, he must like you." Lyddy repeated his remarks over the sleeping arrangements.

"Goodness, we get to share a room as well? Your dad's very open-minded."

"Yes, he is, in his old age. He says you can put it down to losing his marbles." Lyddy leant over Chris to pick up her drink. "I'll have to watch you two. You'll be ganging up on me and making my life miserable. He's probably preparing his best embarrassing stories to throw past you to make me squirm. Just refuse if he offers to get the photo albums out."

Chris lay on her back, looking up at Lyddy, studying her face, "I'm going to tell my mum and dad about you. When I go and stay with them." She put on a wry face, "They won't be such a pushover as your dad."

"Do you want to tell them? Yet, I mean."

"Yes, I do. I've thought about it. They'll have to meet you some time. I just want to give them a chance to get used to the idea first."

"How are they likely to take it?"

"Badly, I imagine," Chris replied, matter-of-factly. "Don't worry, I can manage."

Lyddy put her drink down. She slipped her hand under Chris's sweatshirt to find her bare skin. "Do you find it a bit daunting?"

Chris's expression acknowledged that she did, but she added, "There's no alternative, is there? We've got to go through it, that's all. I'm sure there's a light at the end of the tunnel." She squeezed Lyddy's hand through her sweatshirt. "You'll have to meet this friend of mine, Maggie," she said.

"The one you're going to see before Easter?"

"Mm. She's my oldest friend. We've known each other since University. She got married for the second time in December; I haven't seen her since then. She's got a little girl from her first marriage. You'll like her. You're very alike. She takes everything calmly and on face value, without casting judgement."

"What will she say about you and me?"

"She'll probably say something like, 'Bloody Hell,' think about it and then ask if I'm in love with you and I'll say yes and she'll ask when she can meet you and she'll probably invite us up for a weekend."

Chris watched for Lyddy's reaction.

Lyddy looked down at her, taking in the admission she had just made. "Are you?" she asked softly. "Just like that?"

"Yes," Chris returned Lyddy's look, "I am." There was no more to be said.

Lyddy felt a surge of happiness, a physical thing. "I like a woman who knows what she wants," she said.

"Don't make fun of me," Chris said lightly. "I'm not your sister."

"Thank God for that." The corners of her mouth started to turn up.

Chris let out a groan. "Oh, I see. This is how it's going to be."

"What *are* you talking about."

"The butt of your humour."

"Talking of butts," Lyddy had to laugh now.

"Amazing how people show their true colours on intimate acquaintance, isn't it?"

"Nothing like it. Nothing like intimate acquaintance either."

Chris gazed into Lyddy's eyes, looking from one to the other across the short distance between their faces.

The laughter still showed in Lyddy's face, "Those dreamy come to bed eyes."

"Lyddy?"

"Hm?"

"Be serious."

"Right. I'll try."

Chris let Lyddy's bantering tone go over her head. Her voice was a whisper, "Kiss me."

It got through to Lyddy, her body stirring in response. She pushed her knee between Chris's legs, and held her face close to hers, "Mmm... long and slow."

Chris fumbled for a moment, undoing the button to loosen Lyddy's waistband, then moved her body to press against her. She put her arms around her, sliding her hands down the back of Lyddy's jeans as they kissed. She spoke softly with their mouths together, "How discreet do we have to be?"

In reply, Lyddy pressed her mouth down hard on Chris's and rolled over on top of her.

Chapter Twelve

The following Saturday, Lyddy stopped the car outside Chris's house. She had treated herself to a quick dash to the shops during lunch the day before. She wore a loose navy collarless jacket and skirt in lightweight linen, and a silver-grey silk vest. She felt good.

She grinned to herself as she walked up the path; she'd been looking forward to this. She wiped the grin off her face as Chris opened the door to her knock. "You look lovely," Chris said as she put her arms out. "Mm... you smell nice, too."

"So do you." Lyddy kissed her, "You look good enough to eat." She laughed. "I seem to be developing cannibalistic tendencies. I like your dress, what there is of it." Chris wore a black wool tunic dress ending half way down her thigh, black stockings and a plain gold necklace with dangling earrings. Lyddy slipped her arms round her, "Let's not go out. I've changed my mind."

Chris laughed and kissed her mouth, "You're not ripping this off yet, after all the trouble I've been to. Anyway, I'm starving. Let's go." She went through to the kitchen, locked up the back of the house and pulled Lyddy out through the front door, putting on her jacket as they walked to the car.

Lyddy rang the bell of flat number five at the main entrance to the apartment block where Will and Carl lived. It was a two storey block of six flats, set in small but secluded, well-tended gardens. A buzzer sounded and Lyddy pushed the outer door open when she heard the click. They took the wide stairs arm-in-arm to the first floor. A large gilt-framed mirror dominated the landing area; a beautiful Chinese vase stood on a low walnut table by the lift. The thick carpeting gave noticeably under their feet.

"This looks very plush," Chris commented.

"The trappings of success." Lyddy stepped forward to press the door bell.

The door opened before she touched the bell and Carl's smiling face appeared. He was taller than Will, fair-haired, a youthful face for his forty-two years. He put his arms out, "Lyddy, my darling. I haven't seen you for ages." He hugged her for a few moments. "Are we going to get you drunk tonight?"

"No, Carl. I'm driving. I decided to stay sober for once."

She started to turn to introduce Chris who had come in behind her but Will appeared through the doorway leading from the lounge. He came up to Lyddy and kissed her cheek, squeezing her shoulders. "Hello, sweetheart. It's lovely to see you." He let go of Lyddy and smiled at Chris, "Hello. Good! The more the merrier." He took a step to glance out of the open doorway onto the landing. "Where's Chris? Did he chicken out?" he asked as he turned back to the others in the hall.

Chris stared at him for a second or two, then understood. She laughed and flashed a look at Lyddy, "Christ, Lyddy!"

Lyddy stared impassively at her and raised her eyebrows in mock inquiry. Will was looking from one to the other questioningly.

Chris put out her hand. "You must be Will. I'm Chris," she said.

Will's face registered confusion then disbelief. He looked towards Lyddy as if for confirmation and she smiled beatifically at him, saying nothing. He took Chris's hand and gazed at her; he couldn't find the words. Still holding her hand Will tossed his head back and laughed, glanced at Lyddy and back to Chris again. "I'm gob-smacked!" he said and leant forward to kiss her. He looked across at Lyddy; admiration mixed with amazement at her hoax. Then he smiled back at Chris and leant to kiss her cheek a second time, "And I'm glad to meet you."

Lyddy couldn't help looking pleased with herself. Will stepped across to her and put one arm round her shoulders. "You cow!" He was still incredulous.

"Thank you, darling," she answered demurely.

Carl had been watching, enjoying the scene. He took Chris's hand, "I'm Carl. It's very nice to have you here. Take no notice of Will. I think he left his manners in his coat pocket." He steered Chris towards the lounge, "Let me take your coat and get you a drink. You are drinking, I hope? If you're a friend of Lyddy's, you must drink. We'll leave Will to wreak his revenge on her. This will take him some time to get over."

Chris went through to the lounge with him, smiling broadly. She had enjoyed it all, too.

Will stood with his arm still round Lyddy's shoulders. He put his head on one side and flung her a wry, dry look. "Very clever, my love. What do you do for an encore?"

"Will, I don't know what you mean! I never said…"

She didn't finish. Will grabbed her by the shoulders and pulled her to him to hug her, "No, quite. Bloody hell, Lyddy!"

She had to laugh with him. She couldn't keep it up any longer. "I told you I'd get you back."

"Bloody hell," he said again. "Come on, I need a drink." They followed Chris and Carl into the lounge.

Some three hours later, they all sat in the lounge. Will, Carl and Chris had all drunk too much. They'd had a wonderful meal of crispy duck and a roast caramel cake with cream. Carl had trained as a chef in his younger days before he turned his hand to something more lucrative.

Lyddy sat on the sofa, Chris beside her leaning on her shoulder, holding out her brandy glass which Will was topping up. Lyddy didn't mind not drinking. It was a special night for her and she had enjoyed savouring it sober. It was also entertaining to watch the three of them getting drunk.

Will, of course, had wanted to know how she and Chris had come together, along with all the details he could wrangle from them. He even asked them who had made the first move.

"Mind your own damn business," Lyddy told him.

Carl had laughed. "For God's sake, Will. Enough!" He looked across the table at Chris, "You'll have to forgive him. He thinks he has the market on Lyddy's life and welfare. You'll get used to it."

They had talked of other things over the meal: Will's case in court, Carl's business. They got on to politics. Carl had nearly lost everything during the recent recession and spoke heatedly of the government in power.

"To think, Carl," said Lyddy, "you were once such a staunch Tory."

Carl grinned. "I'm definitely a staunch Tory has-been these days."

"You couldn't be much else with your life-style," Lyddy remarked dryly.

"Well, you can talk." Carl looked pointedly between her and Chris.

Lyddy smiled. "I was never a true-blue."

"Not in politics, anyway," Carl responded.

They discussed the likely repercussions of the next election, though not yet due, Carl indicating he had even worse misgivings for them all with this government gone. In the end he had shrugged his shoulders, "Let's change the subject, this is too depressing."

They talked about Peter's accident and their invitation to Lyddy's father's at Easter. They laughed at Annie's reaction to Lyddy and Chris. Will and Carl asked Chris about herself and they talked about teaching.

They got on to the other tenants in the luxury apartment block. Carl was almost poetic in the pictures he portrayed of their neighbours – the way they politely side-stepped, with typical, well-bred English reserve, the issue of the two men living together in the block. It was amusing, but undoubtedly better than open hostility.

Will told them about their planned holiday, a month in Italy. Will was something of a collector of Italian art, the walls of the apartment showing off his collection, vases and sculptures adorning the furniture and fireplace.

In the end, they sat in the lounge, Chris and Carl exchanging jokes. Chris had a string of nun jokes. Carl's last had them in fits, one about the Twenty Questions radio show with Lady Isobel Barnett on the panel, the object animal with abstract connections.

Chris got up to go to the bathroom and Will came over to sit by Lyddy. He put his arm round her. "So much for not wanting a lover," he said. "She's lovely, Lyddy."

"I know."

"I'm really happy for you."

Lyddy leant her head on his shoulder. "Thank you."

"I'm still slightly gob-smacked. I never imagined it of you."

"No, neither did I. Your face was a picture, if I may say so."

"Ha!" He cocked his head at her, grinning, "Does this mean you can still be a feminist? In the true sense of the word, of course. Not a rejecter of men, per se."

"Don't be sarcastic. And yes it does."

"Except you won't be labelled."

"No, I won't be labelled."

"In case it's misconstrued."

"In case it's misconstrued," she laughed. "Doesn't this annoy you?" she asked Carl. "This knack he has of remembering past conversations verbatim?"

Carl smiled, "Don't knock it. It's making him a wealthy man."

Will turned his head to look at Lyddy, the joking aside. "Where's this going to lead, then?" he wondered.

"I don't know, Will. Chris has just been offered a deputy head's job near Oxford, to start in September."

"Oh, Lyddy!" Will let out a sigh. He met her eye for a moment.

'He's thinking I'm going to get hurt,' thought Lyddy.

Will said, "Will you cope?"

Lyddy looked sorrowfully at him; she didn't hide things from Will. "I don't know. We don't have much choice, do we?"

Will squeezed her shoulder. "A weekend relationship. Oh, Lyddy!" he said again.

Chris came back into the room and Lyddy smiled up at her, "Shall we make a move?"

They made a firm date for Will and Carl to come to Lyddy's, settling on a Saturday in a month's time. As they left, Carl walked Lyddy out through the door of the apartment. Will hung back to give Chris a hug and say again how pleased he was to meet her. He stepped back, holding Chris at arm's length. "Don't hurt her, will you?" It was a request. He was a little drunk but genuinely concerned after talking to Lyddy.

Chris looked bewildered, "No! Nothing could be further from my mind." She paused, she was more than a little tipsy but she had only just met Will this evening. "I'm not playing games, Will."

"Good. I'm sorry." Will hugged her again and she and Lyddy left.

As they drove home, Chris said, "Will's very fond of you, isn't he?"

Lyddy laughed, "Yes, he is." She glanced at Chris as she drove, "Was he giving you a hard time?"

"I don't know." She took Lyddy's hand which was resting on the gear lever. "He told me not to hurt you."

"Oh, Chris, I'm sorry. It's well-meant. Don't be too bothered by it."

Chris was silent for a few moments, then she said, "Lyddy, I won't hurt you."

Lyddy glanced at her again, "I know. I'm not the one who's worried. Cheer up! Did you enjoy the evening?"

"Yes, I did. They're good fun." She sounded cheerful again. "You really pulled a fast one, didn't you?"

Lyddy just laughed as she pulled up outside Chris's house and switched off the engine. They got out of the car and walked to the front door in the dark, with their arms round each other.

Chris tucked her head into Lyddy's shoulder and kissed her neck. "Booze makes me very amorous when I'm with you. Well, more so, I should say."

"I've noticed," Lyddy answered. "I find it a very endearing quality in you. I'm going to exploit it to the full."

"What? Take advantage of me?"

"Absolutely."

Chris unlocked the door and kicked it shut behind them. She linked arms with Lyddy. "Let's not bother with coffee, then," she said. They walked upstairs, laughing as they struggled two abreast to get up the narrow stairway.

Chapter Thirteen

A rug was spread out on the grass, the remains of the picnic scattered on it. Lyddy sat on a corner of the rug, resting her back against a tree stump. She lifted her face to the sun, eyes closed, listening to the sounds coming from the river: the cries of the children, her dad's shout, Chris's laugh.

For April, the weather was warm. The children had taken off their sweatshirts and discarded their shoes and socks. The odd, white fluffy cloud hung in the sky, otherwise it was a clear blue. The hedges, fields and trees stretched away beyond the river, a tractor monotonously grinding up and down one of the fields.

It was Good Friday. They had arrived the afternoon before, in time for tea. The children were excited; they'd all sung songs in the car, laughing as they got muddled up singing the rounds. They'd played word games, then made up silly rhymes about people they knew. Lyddy was voted the winner at this. The children learnt her best one by heart to tell their grandad,

"There was a young lady called Nikki,
Who suddenly felt a bit sicky.
She said to her mum,
'Look what I've done.
Oh, it's gone! The dog's had a licky!'"

Lyddy smiled as she remembered the journey. They had all been in a very silly mood by the time they reached her father's house. He had a salad tea laid out in readiness when they got there. The children went out into the garden to reconnoitre their favourite play areas and her dad took Lyddy and Chris upstairs with the luggage. He stopped at the door to the main bedroom, his eyes twinkling. "I'm afraid you're in here. I moved into the twin room at the back when I decorated. I prefer the view of the river." He showed them into the room, the five foot double bed still there which he had shared with Lyddy's mum, the en-suite bathroom leading off.

They put their luggage on the bed and Lyddy's dad turned to Chris as he said, "I hope you'll be alright. It's a comfortable bed."

"I'm sure we'll be fine. Thank you." Chris grinned at him, marvelling at his broad-mindedness.

He left them and went back downstairs to call the children in for tea. After he'd gone, Chris raised her eyebrows at Lyddy, finding it hard to believe. Her parents had taken her news very badly. They didn't want to meet Lyddy and, after a while, wouldn't discuss it further. She'd had a very hard two days with them and had reconciled herself to a wait-and-see-and-hope attitude.

Lyddy laughed, to take her out of her thoughts. "I think he *is* losing his marbles," she said. "My mum will be turning in her grave. Mind you," she walked over to where Chris stood and they put their arms round each other, "I intend to take full advantage of his hospitality."

"Oh, good," said Chris. She put her lips against Lyddy's. "I've missed you." They hadn't seen each other since Saturday, Chris had not got back until the evening before.

"I've given Peter and Nikki a pep-talk," Lyddy said. She drew her head back so that she could look at Chris as she spoke. "I told them that you would be sharing a room with me so they mustn't come bursting in. They must knock and wait for an answer." She grinned, "You'll have to have your pyjamas on by morning, though; we won't keep them out much after seven o'clock."

"Well, if I'm going to be woken that early, don't keep me awake all night," Chris said. She had put her parents out of her mind.

"You can talk!"

There was a shout from the children at the bottom of the stairs, "Tea's ready!"

Lyddy answered their call and kissed Chris before they went downstairs.

After tea they had played cricket in the garden. Lyddy's dad was umpire and wicket keeper. It was Peter and Lyddy against Nikki and Chris. Peter was somewhat hampered by his plaster cast but he batted one-handed. The garden was enormous. Lyddy's parents had moved into the house twenty years before, when Lyddy left home. The owner before them had built the house himself, buying the land from a local farmer, and he had been free to mark out how much land he wanted. There were two large lawns, broken halfway by a mixture of large shrubs and small trees. There was a small orchard of ten apple trees at the end with an old shed in the bottom corner full of gardening bits and pieces. A gardener came two mornings a week; it was all well-kept.

Chris and Nikki had won the match, much to Nikki's delight, She was too competitive, Lyddy thought. Peter bore his loss with good humour.

After the children had gone to bed, Chris and Lyddy sat talking with her dad. He told Chris about Lyddy's mum, talked about her in a way that he hadn't done since her death. Lyddy was pleased. He had really come to terms with it now. It had taken long enough. She thought how content he seemed. He had joined the local golf club and taken up bowls in the neighbouring, larger village, meeting new people. He had a whole new social life which he had never bothered with when his wife was alive.

They talked through the evening, polishing off a couple of bottles of wine. Chris told Lyddy's dad about herself, her family. He asked her quite openly if her parents knew about Lyddy. Chris made a face. "Yes, they do. I just got back yesterday from staying with them."

"I take it they weren't impressed."

"Yes, you could say that."

"Don't worry," he said. "They'll come round." He smiled at her, "I think you're old enough to make up your own mind, don't you?"

Lyddy looked at him gratefully and Chris answered, "Yes, I do."

They talked a bit longer, deciding on a picnic by the river the next day if it was nice. Lyddy's dad poured them all a brandy and went over to Lyddy to kiss her goodnight, "I'm off to bed now. I'll take this with me."

"Good Lord, Dad. Taking booze to bed with you?"

"It's the prerogative of old age, darling. You do what you like when you like. Mind you," he added as he bent to kiss Chris's cheek, "you two seem to have started young."

"Very funny."

He laughed as he walked to the door and turned with a wicked smile on his face. What now? thought Lyddy.

106

"Not too much noise up there. I'm a light sleeper these days. I'm not too old to remember young love – I don't want to be kept awake all night."

"Oh dear! Go to bed. Don't encourage him," she directed this last at Chris who was laughing at him.

"Goodnight, my loves." He left the room.

After a second brandy, they had got the giggles as they were getting ready for bed later, shushing each other so as not to wake Lyddy's dad. Lyddy was somewhat the worse for the drink she had consumed. She pulled Chris's pyjamas from her open suitcase. "What are these? You'll look like you've escaped from Alcatraz." She held them up against her and started laughing.

Chris grabbed Lyddy's nightshirt from the top of the blanket box, "What about this? You'll look like the man in the toilet paper ad."

They exploded into laughter and the more they tried to keep quiet, the more they laughed. Soon they were laughing at themselves laughing. Chris collapsed into a chair with the night-shirt pressed against her face. She took it away to look at Lyddy and said between breaths, "You're drunk! I'm not sleeping with a drunken woman!"

Lyddy had tears down her cheeks. She controlled herself long enough to feign a serious expression, "Sleep? What makes you think you're going to get any sleep?" The mirth rose up again. She sat on the bed clutching her stomach, "We haven't come here to sleep!"

Chris took the night-shirt away again, "Ssh! We'll wake the children as well. We'll have them all in here in a minute to see what's going on." She burst out laughing again at the mental picture of pyjama-clad, sleepy-eyed figures at the doorway.

Lyddy stood up and forced herself towards the bathroom. If she couldn't see Chris's face, she might get herself under control.

"What are you smiling about?"

Lyddy opened her eyes, shading them from the sun with her hand. Chris was coming towards her. She lay down along the edge of the rug so that her head rested in Lyddy's lap.

"I was thinking about last night," Lyddy said.

Chris glanced down towards the river before she reached behind her for Lyddy's hand and pushed it under her sweater, holding it on her bare skin. "Have you been sitting here having lustful thoughts while I've been down there playing with your children?"

"No. God, you have a one-track mind."

"I thought that's what attracted you to me."

Lyddy shaded her eyes again to focus on the children and slipped her hand just inside Chris's waistband. "I know. It's true. Actually, I was thinking about the pyjamas."

Chris giggled at the memory. It had been so ridiculous. She twisted her neck to look up at Lyddy. "As it turned out, I thought you looked very sexy in your night-shirt."

"Thank you. I thought you felt very sexy in your pyjamas."

"It's a good job we remembered to put them on, isn't it?"

It was. Nikki and Peter had come in just after seven, armed with the biscuit tin and books for stories. Chris had gone downstairs to make tea and drinks and they had all squeezed in, sitting up in the big bed as Lyddy read to the children.

Lyddy put her hand up again to shade her eyes and saw Nikki running towards them. She took her other hand away, pulling the sweater down over Chris's tummy as she did so. Chris stayed where she was with her head in Lyddy's lap.

Nikki came running up, water slopping from her bucket as she ran. "Look, Mum. I've got some tiddlers." She bent down to show Lyddy. "I put some weed in as well, in case they're hungry."

"Lovely, darling. We can have fish for tea."

"Mum! You can't *eat* them. They're too small. Grandad says we have to put them back in the river before we go."

Peter came running up as well. "Hi, Mum! Did you see what we caught? Are we going to play hide and seek now?"

There was a copse of trees and bushes off to their left, perfect for the game. Lyddy had promised them. "Okay, sweetheart. Have a drink first. Is Grandad playing?"

Her father was following them up the slope at a more leisurely pace, carrying their socks and trainers and fishing nets.

"No, he says he's going to have forty winks."

"That's not much, is it?" Nikki sat back on her haunches, blinking as she counted.

"It doesn't mean forty winks, dummy."

"Peter, please don't call her that."

Peter went on, "It's just what you say, isn't it, Mum? Forty winks. It means a sleep."

"I know that, I was just counting. You don't know everything, you know."

"Oh, you two! Have your drinks and put your shoes on and we'll go and play hide and seek. You'll have to pull me up, I think I've taken root with this tree stump."

They laughed and giggled as they tried to pull her up, Lyddy making herself a dead weight and falling over on her side in the grass. They enlisted Chris's help and got her to her feet and all went off to play the game, leaving Lyddy's father to have a nap in peace.

Lyddy put the car into gear and moved forward a few yards before putting it into neutral again and pulling up the handbrake. There was probably an accident ahead. It was just getting dark. She could see the trail of red tail-lights stretching up as far as the top of the rise, half a mile ahead, not knowing how far beyond that the jam went.

She sighed impatiently. Bank Holiday traffic. This is what she had hoped to avoid. They had decided to leave her father's after tea, hoping they would miss most of the traffic but the weather had been so glorious that everyone else had left it till late to go home as well.

The children were asleep in the back, Peter snoring quietly. They were worn out from the weekend. Chris had nodded off too.

Lyddy glanced ruefully in the rear mirror at the line of lights in the queue of traffic behind her. They could have stayed another night, leaving the next morning, but Peter had his appointment at the hospital to have his plaster cast taken off.

She inched the car forward again. She thought what a wonderful weekend they had just had. They had taken a rowing boat down the river, visited a country park which had an enormous adventure playground for the children. They'd had a picnic out somewhere each day and, she thought, they'd had such a lot of laughs. Her dad had made them promise to come up again during the summer holidays.

Lyddy looked across at Chris. She had reclined her seat a little, her head resting on the back of it. Even in the dim light, Lyddy could see the healthy glow of her skin from being out in the sun each day. She felt a rush of emotion. Being with Chris each night had been the icing on the cake of the weekend. She wasn't looking forward to dropping her off when they got back. "God, she's lovely," she thought, and reached over to hold one of Chris's hands lying in her lap.

Chris squeezed Lyddy's hand, "I'm not asleep." She turned her head as she spoke, opening her eyes. "I was thinking."

"What about?" Lyddy asked, keeping her voice low although the children would barely wake up enough to get into bed when they got home.

Chris was silent for a moment, keeping her eyes on Lyddy. "About what a wonderful weekend it's been; how much I love being with you; how much I'm going to miss you tonight; what a laugh we've had, and," she heaved a sigh, "how I'm going to cope, living up there after the summer." She made a face, trying to find some humour somewhere. She couldn't. "Is that enough to be going on with?" She watched Lyddy, a sad expression on her face, looking to her for an answer.

Lyddy took a deep breath, reflecting on this. She squeezed Chris's hand before letting it go to roll the car forward again, then put her hand back on Chris's. She didn't answer straight away, contemplating her own feelings. Then she rallied herself, "Look on the bright side. You can catch up on some sleep tonight." She couldn't help the grin.

Chris rolled her eyes upwards in exasperation.

"Sorry," Lyddy was chastened. "It's just as bad for me, you know. Leaving you at your house tonight." She glanced at Chris, "I'm going to miss you too."

Chris pushed herself more upright in her seat and stared through the windscreen. "Lyddy, I shouldn't have taken that job. I knew it at the time but it was too soon to have made such a decision. I shouldn't have taken it," she said again.

"But you did take it, you can't change that now." They were interviewing after the Easter holidays to replace Chris at the school, and she couldn't withdraw her acceptance of her new post now.

Lyddy continued in a positive vein, "It will be alright. We'll come up to you for weekends. You'll come down to us. And we have long holidays."

Chris wrinkled her nose, unhappy at the prospect but knowing she would have to accept it.

Lyddy found inspiration, hoping to shake Chris out of this, "Shall we book a holiday for the summer? The four of us, I mean."

It had the desired effect. "Yes, that would be lovely. Where were you thinking of?"

"I don't know. Somewhere where there are things for the children to do. Near a beach, maybe. Rent a cottage or something. I haven't thought any further than that."

Chris squeezed her hand, recovering some of her cheerfulness. "As long as it's a cottage with a double bed."

Lyddy smiled at her, "Of course, that goes without saying. We'll make it a fortnight. Just think – two whole weeks together."

"That sounds wonderful."

"It does, doesn't it?" Lyddy turned her thoughts to the coming week. "Are you doing anything on Thursday?"

Chris looked to her to explain.

"Well, Annie and Bob are taking the children to Longleat for the day and they're staying the night at Annie's. I could come over and stay."

Chris grinned at her now, feeling silly to have got so morose. "Great. I look forward to it."

"Can I bring Dodger? I can't keep asking Mr Burberry to have him."

"Of course you can." Chris reached her hand over to rest on Lyddy's leg. "I'm sorry," she said, referring to her melancholy moment. "I can't help it sometimes. It was such a lovely weekend and I don't want it to end." She rubbed her hand on Lyddy's leg to make her point. "I've never felt like this before, you know."

Lyddy looked at her. "No, nor have I," she said, with some surprise at the realisation. "You'll talk yourself back into it if you're not careful."

Chris grinned. "You're a hard woman."

"Good job one of us is."

"And you're always taking the piss out of me," Chris affected a churlish tone, regaining her equilibrium.

"Well, you make it so easy for me."

"Ha! Ha!"

Lyddy laughed out loud. Then she said, "You didn't tell me how your visit with Maggie went." They hadn't had that much time over the weekend to sit and talk to each other.

"It was just as I told you it would be." Chris grinned again. "You're so alike. She took the mickey out of me most of the two days I was there. I don't think I should let you two get together."

Lyddy looked over at Chris to see if she was going to go on.

She did. "We're invited up at half term. She wants to meet you. She said to bring the children as well."

"Goodness, she's brave. Say yes, I'd like that. What's her husband like?"

Chris went on to tell Lyddy about Maggie and Tony and how she had spent her time with them. As they talked, the traffic started moving more quickly. They eventually got back to normal speed but didn't see any sign of what had held them up. Presumably everything had been cleared away by the time they got there.

They eventually arrived at Chris's house and Lyddy went in with her for a few minutes. It was dark now, the children still asleep in the car. When Lyddy drove off, she felt strangely alone and thought about their arrangements for the coming week to shake the feeling off.

Chapter Fourteen

The weeks of the summer term flew past, busily and eventfully.

They had Will and Carl over on several occasions and went out for meals with them, always guaranteed a good evening. Will had relaxed his concern for Lyddy, seeing how close she and Chris were growing. They had even been invited to Annie and Bob's for dinner, not one of their dinner parties, just the four of them. Annie was making the effort she had promised; she made Chris welcome and admitted to Lyddy that she liked her. She didn't allow herself to dwell too much on what they got up to in private, though.

They all went to stay at Maggie's at half-term. As Chris had predicted, Lyddy and Maggie got on like a house on fire. Chris had to endure their jokes at her expense nearly every time she opened her mouth and she threatened to go home on the train. The children found a new playmate in Laura, Maggie's seven year old. Of Chris's friends, only Maggie really accepted their affair. Anne, another close friend, was very ill at ease on the one occasion that she met Lyddy.

Lyddy's friend, Jane, had seen Chris at the house several times over the weeks. One morning, sitting at the kitchen table having a coffee with her, Lyddy mentioned that Chris was coming on holiday with her and the children. Jane eyed her shrewdly, holding her cup to her mouth, "I might be barking up the wrong tree, but is this what I think it is?" Lyddy looked at her and she added, "You and Chris Carter."

Lyddy smiled and said, "Yes, probably."

Jane's eyes widened a little, "Gosh." It was delivered in a level voice, a deliberate understatement. She could be very droll at times.

Lyddy laughed, "I wondered; had you guessed before?"

"Well, no, not really. But I did think there must be some sort of extra-curricular activity going on." She sat in silence for a few seconds, drinking her coffee. Then she said, "How exciting!" and grinned at Lyddy. "I'm almost envious."

She included Chris in the invitation to her fortieth birthday party in June.

Chris's parents remained stubborn in their attitude to their daughter's relationship with another woman. Chris went to visit them once during the term and they spent a night at her cottage on another occasion. Lyddy stayed away; there was no question of them meeting her. Her mother's words to Chris were, "You're embarrassing us by even suggesting it. I have no wish to meet that woman." Chris was upset but had to accept her feelings. She felt it would be too hard on them all to fall out over it.

Annie decided to take the bull by the horns and invited Lyddy and Chris to her twentieth wedding anniversary party. It was an elaborate but tasteful affair. Annie thought she dealt with the odd question from her friends, about her sister, with remarkable decorum, and she thanked Lyddy after the event for behaving themselves. Lyddy swallowed a cynical reply and told Annie she was welcome.

Peter and Nikki blithely accepted Chris staying the odd night here and there. As there was no bed in the spare room it was natural that she shared Lyddy's bed as she had at their grandad's. They liked her staying. Apart from enjoying her presence, they got more stories in the mornings as they all wedged in, filling the bed with biscuit crumbs. Lyddy supposed that she might start to get the odd awkward question from them at some point, but decided to deal with them when and if they came.

The children got their rabbits, named Twitch and Spit, because, they said, that's what they do. Peter's twitched its nose all the time and Nikki's appeared to spit at them. Lyddy thought it was just poking the tip of its tongue out but Nikki was adamant, "No, he's spitting."

Chris and Lyddy spent Chris's thirty-sixth birthday in a cottage in the heart of Dorset, away from everything. Annie had offered to have the children for the weekend if they wanted "to do something special". Lyddy marvelled at her. She was more than making an effort. Lyddy's father said that Annie had commented on how happy Lyddy was these days and, he said, "The rest takes its course, doesn't it?"

And all the other things of course, the day to day routine, that fills the weeks and makes the time seem to pass so quickly: getting everyone to school in the morning, marking, planning work for school, parents evenings, trips out at weekends.

The term had just gone, Lyddy thought, almost in a whirl. She was weary from it but happy, glad that the holidays were here.

She was kneeling on the floor of her bedroom, with all the children's summer clothes in front of her, sorting them out. Nikki and Peter were in bed. It was a balmy summer evening outside. It was Thursday; the schools had broken up the day before for the holidays. They were leaving on Saturday, Lyddy, Chris and the children. They had booked a small house for two weeks in Port Isaac, a little fishing village along the coast of North Cornwall. They discussed Brittany and decided to stay in this country. The weather had been mostly good since Easter and the long-term forecast was promising. As far as Brittany was concerned, they were just as much at the mercy of the weather there as here.

Lyddy loved Cornwall. She had spent holidays there as a child and was looking forward to going back. The children would love the beaches, the surf, the rock pools.

Her thoughts were broken by the sound of someone coming up the stairs. She stopped what she was doing and looked towards the door.

"Hello, my darling," Chris walked into the room with a smile. "I came in through the back door. It was open."

Lyddy straightened her back and put her face up to Chris. She came over and bent to put her arms round Lyddy to kiss her. Lyddy smiled, always happy to see her. "Have you just got back?" she asked.

"Yes. I went home to change and came straight round." She was wearing shorts and a sleeveless T-shirt.

Lyddy looked down at herself. She just had an old T-shirt and knickers on. She laughed, "We have to go naked till Saturday. Everything's going in the wash."

"Oh, good. I'm glad I'm staying." Chris sat down on the bed, close to Lyddy, kicked her sandals off and pulled her legs up in front of her, hugging them with her arms.

"How did it go?" Lyddy asked as she picked up more clothes. Chris had been up to her new school for the day. They broke up a day later up there, so she was able to spend the day seeing the headmistress and getting acquainted with the school.

"It went well. I met all the other staff. They seem a nice bunch. I had a good look round the school, had a long talk to the Head. It was worth the trip. I ended up having tea with the retiring deputy." Chris looked pleased with herself. "She's offered me her house to rent for next term."

Lyddy looked up in surprise for Chris to explain.

"She's going to Suffolk to look after her mother who's waiting to have an operation. She's not sure how long she'll be up there or even if she will stay up there for good. Anyway, she's keeping her house on to see how things go and asked me if I'd like to rent it until I find somewhere else. She's even going to ask her cleaner if she'll stay on for me."

"What's it like?"

"A bit big, but nice. She's not charging me much. She wants someone living in it while she's gone." Chris shrugged, "It saves me dashing around up there looking for somewhere to live. It's only about fifteen minutes drive from school."

"When is she going to Suffolk?"

"She's going straight up there now. I told her I couldn't move in until the weekend before term starts. She seemed happy with that." Chris put her head on one side and made a face at Lyddy. Talking about it brought it closer but they seemed to have a silent pact now, not to dwell on it, at least not openly. They had the summer holidays to look forward to.

Lyddy tossed the last T-shirt onto the pile and sat back on her heels. She reached out a hand to rub Chris's bare leg. "Good. I'm glad it was a successful day. Do you fancy a drink?"

"Mm. Gasping for one."

Lyddy stood up. "We can take it out in the garden. I must check on the rabbits, make sure they've been fed."

Chris let her legs down over the side of the bed and held a hand out to Lyddy. She took it and Chris pulled her on to the bed next to her, so that they were lying on their sides, facing each other. "I want a hug first."

They kissed and Chris ran her hand over Lyddy's body, over her T-shirt. "You've got no bra on."

"It's in the wash." Lyddy smiled at her, sensing what was coming.

Chris grinned back, "Mm..." She pushed Lyddy over on to her back and moved so that she was sitting astride her tummy. She pulled Lyddy's T-shirt up as far as it would go under her arm-pits. "Take this off." Lyddy crossed her arms, pulled the T-shirt over her head, whirled it around in the air a couple of times and tossed it away. Chris pushed herself backwards off the bed, pulled Lyddy's pants off and threw her own clothes aside as she took them off. Then she slowly slid herself up Lyddy's body until she was lying full length over her. Lyddy wrapped her arms and legs around her and they rolled over as one, opening their mouths onto each other.

Saturday morning found them all packed up, in the car and on the road by ten o'clock which, Lyddy thought, was a miracle. Dodger had gone to Mr Burberry's for his holiday; the rabbits had gone to Jane's children for theirs and Lyddy had gone nearly mad trying to contain the children's excitement while they were all getting ready.

It was the first Saturday of the school holidays, supposedly the busiest day of the year. They hit heavy traffic almost straight away, but they kept moving and speeded up after they got past Bridport along the south coast. Chris had packed some sandwiches and drinks, so, apart from a toilet stop, they kept going and stopped for a break and a late lunch once they were past Exeter. Lyddy felt they were getting somewhere at last, more open country. They had left the heavy traffic behind them.

At four o'clock, they were finally on the twisting lanes heading for the north coast, all marvelling at the narrowness of them and the steepness of the hills.

"I hope the tide's out," Lyddy said. "If it is, they use the harbour as a car park."

"What happens when the tide comes in again?" Peter asked.

"Well, you have to make sure you move your car before it does. They put a sign up telling you when you have to be back by."

"Will we park in the harbour, Mum?" It was Nikki's question.

"No, we don't need to. There's a parking space at the house."

She drove slowly down the narrow street towards the harbour with "Oohs" and "Aahs" from the children at the sight of the sea, the harbour, the fishing boats. The tide was about halfway in, a few cars still parked up on the bit of beach at the top.

"I hope we don't meet anyone," Lyddy said to Chris as she manoeuvred the car round a sharp bend. The house on the corner had obviously taken a few knocks in the small space. Big lumps of plaster were missing from its corner walls.

They found the street they wanted, whitewashed terraces, and Lyddy pulled the car off the road under the archway which went through to the garden at the back. She got out and went across the street to get the keys of the house, as she had been instructed.

The children tumbled through the door when she opened it, and after a cursory glance at the downstairs rooms, they dashed upstairs to find their bedroom.

Lyddy peered through the kitchen window into the garden. It was very pretty: paving stones, shrubs, hanging baskets, a fish pond. The place heaved with the character of the village. She turned round as Chris came up behind her and they put their arms round each other.

"You look tired," Chris kissed her.

"I'm alright. I don't really like driving long distances. All that concentrating for long periods." They had come in Lyddy's car because it was bigger. "I really ought to get you put on my insurance, so you could drive as well."

"Do you trust me?"

"Of course I trust you." She smiled at her, "What a daft question. Remind me, I'll phone them on Monday."

Chris said, "I'll put the kettle on and then we can have a look round." They stood with their arms around each other, absorbing the stillness after the drive. They could hear voices and thuds from the children upstairs, then the sound of feet coming down the stairs.

"Mum! There's a balcony upstairs. You can see the harbour from it. Can we have that bedroom?" Peter found them in the kitchen. Chris reached for the kettle.

"I don't know, sweetheart. Let's go and look."

Peter led the way. The sun was streaming in through the open French windows, the view from the large, square balcony looking across the rooftops. Lyddy could see the harbour between two houses; there were rocks to one side and boats of all sizes tied up.

"Can we go and explore the harbour, Mum?" Nikki was standing on the bottom of the railing which ran round the edge of the balcony, leaning over double to look at the fish pond.

"Nikki! Don't do that, it might not be very strong."

Nikki didn't move. Lyddy pulled her upright and said sternly, "*Don't* lean over like that!"

"Can we go and explore?"

"Well, maybe Chris might walk you down there while I get something to eat. After we've unloaded the car," she warned, "and let her have a cup of tea first."

They went back into the bedroom. Lyddy looked around: the sunlight, painted rough walls, dark beams across the ceiling, a beautiful patchwork quilt on the bed. It's wonderful, she thought, just what she had hoped.

"Can we have this bedroom, Mum?"

"No, sweetheart. If you and Nikki share a bed you'll keep each other awake all night. The other room's got two beds in it."

"But that room's dark! It's got no balcony."

"Yes, but you'll get the sun in the morning and I don't trust Nikki on the balcony. She'll be falling off into the fish pond."

Chris came into the room. "Tea's made," she said. "There's milk and stuff in the fridge. What a lovely room." She went out onto the balcony and came back into the bedroom. "It's perfect."

She took Nikki's hand, "Come on, show me where you're sleeping."

Nikki led the way. "The bathroom hasn't got a bath in it," she said. "It's only got a shower."

Chris poked her head round the door of the bathroom. "Well, when these houses were built, they didn't have baths. They didn't even have taps. They put a shower in because there's not enough room for a bath."

"Can we have a shower tonight, Mum?"

"Of course you can."

"Oh, good. I'll wear my goggles."

"Come on," Lyddy said. "We'll have a cup of tea and then get the stuff out of the car."

As they went downstairs, Peter said, "Chris, you're taking me and Nikki to look at the harbour."

"Oh, I am, am I?"

"Yes. Can we get some fudge? Mummy said they sell lovely fudge here."

"I love fudge," Chris told him. "And Cornish cream teas. We'll all get fat and spotty this holiday."

Chapter Fifteen

Lyddy sat with her head resting on the high arm of the sofa, her back propped with cushions, her knees drawn up. Chris lay on her back between Lyddy's legs, her head resting on the soft part of Lyddy's abdomen. It was just getting dark outside, the street lights across the road showing through the small latticed window. Chris was holding the map up in front of her, peering at it in the light from the single lamp they had on behind the sofa. Her bare arms were brown now from being out in the sun every day. They were all sun-tanned; the weather had been kind to them all week. Lyddy was having to plaster the children with sun cream every couple of hours and she had to nag Nikki to keep her hat on.

Elkie Brooks was playing on the stereo. They had been discussing what they would do the next day. They'd had only one cloudy day so far and had spent that on a farm where the children had horse rides, fed the pigs, watched the cows being milked and played on the trampolines in the play area. They'd spent all or part of the other days on different beaches. The children were loving it; playing on the surf board in the waves; filling their buckets with crabs and shrimps in the rock pools; having sand castle competitions; playing ball games on the sand. Lyddy decided she would have to go on a diet when she got home. They'd had ice creams every day and clotted cream teas on three occasions so far. Chris's waistline hadn't seemed to suffer, as far as Lyddy could tell.

She put her drink down on the small table beside her, slipped her hands round Chris's neck and rubbed her shoulders under the straps of her sleeveless T-shirt. She closed her eyes. "I'd like to freeze this moment," she murmured.

Chris threw the map on the floor, finished the last mouthful of her drink and relaxed her head on Lyddy's tummy. She rubbed her hands gently up and down Lyddy's shins. "I think this is the best holiday I've ever had," she said.

"What, better than Crete, Venice, California?"

"I wasn't with you then," Chris replied simply.

"That's the nicest thing you've said to me for half an hour," Lyddy told her, eyes still closed.

"I suppose you think that's funny. Don't mock me."

"Perish the thought."

"You always laugh at me because I say what I feel."

"Laugh? Because you wear your heart on your sleeve? Anyway, you thrive on it. You enjoy it."

"I do not!" Chris retorted.

"Yes, you do. We both benefit. When I really get you going, you respond by doing nice things to me."

"Do I really?"

Lyddy laughed. Chris hugged Lyddy's legs to her. "Peter's getting good on the surf board," she said. "He stood up a couple of times today."

"I know. I was watching for a while. I'll come in with you tomorrow."

"You have to watch Nikki, don't you? She has no fear."

Lyddy agreed. Nikki was a little reckless sometimes. "It's a good job she wears her armbands."

Chris said, "I told her I wouldn't take her in the water unless she did, because of the waves."

Lyddy smiled appreciatively, "You're good with them, aren't you?"

Chris shrugged slightly, accepting the compliment. "They do wear me out, though," she said. "They just keep going till they drop into bed, don't they?"

"I thought you'd be used to them."

"It's different in school, more ordered. And in school it doesn't start at seven in the morning and last till their bedtime."

"Do you mind?" Lyddy asked.

"No, of course not."

Her head still laid back, her eyes still closed, Lyddy said, "I must say, sometimes it would be nice to have half a day off. Holidays with children are not always very restful."

Chris scoffed lightly, "You had nearly half a day off this afternoon! I was in the sea with them for about two hours, while you slept in the sun! That seems pretty restful to me."

"That was only about half a hour." Lyddy waited for the reaction.

"It was not! And then we didn't wake you up when we came out. We went and sat on the rocks to warm up. Peter told Nikki that you work hard and need your sleep."

"Oh, the little darling. I'm bringing him up well."

"When do I get my half-day off?"

Lyddy squeezed Chris's shoulders. "Tomorrow, my love. You can fall asleep in the sun after lunch and I will take the children to catch a crab for tea in the rock pools."

"I'll have to make sure you don't lie down after you've eaten, then."

"Why?"

"Well, you just go out like a light. One minute you're sitting up talking to us and the next you've made a pillow out of something, made yourself prone and," Chris snapped her fingers, "you're gone."

"Is that what I do?"

"After lunch, you do."

"It's the sun and the sound of the surf. It must mean I'm really relaxed, benefiting from the holiday." Lyddy smiled, her eyes still closed, "Maybe it would help if you didn't keep pestering me in the night."

"I do not pester you in the night."

"You do."

Chris gave in and she felt for her glass on the floor. "Do you want another drink?"

"No, let's go to bed." Lyddy moved her hands down the front of Chris's T-shirt and squeezed her gently.

Chris arched her back slightly in response, contentment in her voice as she said, "You're a hypocrite, you know. You're as bad as me, for all your accusations."

"I know. I'm just more subtle about it."

"Oh, very! About as subtle as a hedgehog down your knickers."

Lyddy laughed. "Let's go to bed."

They decided not to go to the beach the next day, but went mackerel fishing instead. They drove down to Padstow and went out on one of the boats running regular trips from the harbour.

On the journey out the children were excitedly predicting who would catch the most fish. When they got out past the headland,

Lyddy had a sharp reminder of what a bad sea traveller she was. "Tell that man to turn this boat around," she told Chris.

Chris was bent down trying to work a hook out of the seat of Nikki's shorts. She turned her head to look at Lyddy, "What?"

"I want to get off. I need to be sick."

"Oh, no!" Chris got the hook out and sat back on the seat next to her. "Think positive. It's mind over matter."

"Easy for you to say." Lyddy lunged across Chris's lap and grabbed Nikki's life-jacket as she tipped just a little too far for comfort to trail her fingers in the water. "Nikki! Keep your bottom on the seat!"

Chris took a firm hold of Nikki's arm and Lyddy let go of the life-jacket. She concentrated on going with the motion of the boat like seating a horse in a canter and let Chris help the children unhook the fish when they pulled their lines in. Towards the end of the trip, as they chugged back towards the land, the others got the packed lunch out. There was a bit of a swell now and the boat was heaving in a sideways, circular motion. Lyddy hoped for the tenth time that she wasn't going to embarrass herself, her nausea almost overwhelming. Breathe deeply. Face into the wind.

Chris held a sandwich out to her, grinning, "Lunch?"

Lyddy closed her eyes to the sight and directed her voice towards Chris's ear, away from the woman sitting next to her, "Shall I tell you what you can do with that?"

"What's up? Not hungry?"

Lyddy opened her eyes again, closing them had made her feel worse. "I didn't know you had a sadistic streak in you."

One of those fast, top-heavy cruisers went across their bow, the men in the cockpit preparing heavy-duty rods for a bigger catch. Half a minute later the bow of the little mackerel boat started pounding into the wash as it hit them. Lyddy's stomach came up to hit her throat. Oh, God! She groaned and gave up. She spun round and bent double over the side just in time, her face only inches from the water. She was aware of Nikki who had pushed in between her and Chris and was leaning over the side with her.

"Oh, Mum!"

Lyddy wasn't sure whether Nikki's tone was of exasperation or disgust but didn't care either. Chris passed her a handful of tissues when she finally resumed her seat in the boat. Lyddy wiped her mouth and eyes and blew her nose, glancing at Chris as she did so. "Don't say a word," she warned her. She felt grateful for once for the tact and reserve of the English, noting that all the other passengers were politely averting their eyes, except for one little boy who was pointedly staring at her. She managed a rueful grin when the skipper at the wheel called across, "Don't worry, love. There's always one. As long as you don't do it into the wind."

"Are you alright, Mum?" Peter called across from his seat in the bow.

"Yes, thank you, darling. I will be."

"Great waves, weren't they?"

"Yes, terrific!"

When they finally climbed the steps of the harbour wall, Lyddy could still feel the boat moving under her feet. Nikki and Peter wanted an ice-cream. Chris took Lyddy's elbow and exaggeratedly supported her weight, steering her towards a tea house with tables and chairs outside. "How about a quiet seat in the sun and a nice cup of tea, dear. Settle you down."

"God, you bitch," Lyddy murmured.

Chris laughed. "Language! Go and sit. I'll get the tea and ice-creams." She handed over their bag of fish and the children followed her to the door of the tea house. Lyddy made her way to the only free table, in the corner, and sat down closing her eyes, enjoying the warmth in the sheltered spot. At least seasickness only lasted while you were on the sea; she was starting to feel better already.

Peter and Nikki came out licking enormous cones and sat astride the wall of the small courtyard, watching the harbour. Chris appeared with the tray of tea things, sat down next to Lyddy and looked over at her, "You're three shades of green lighter. Are you feeling better, my darling?"

"Yes. No thanks to you."

"Oh, your wounded pride."

"Oh, arseholes."

Chris snorted. "Lyddy! I see now where your daughter gets her colourful expletives from. To think you tried to blame the school."

Lyddy laughed at this, putting her humiliation away. "Pour me a cup of tea and stop giving me a hard time. I'll have one of those tea cakes too. I'm starving."

"I'm not surprised. You must have left half your stomach back there."

"Yes, don't rub it in."

They sat in the sun facing the courtyard, watching the harbour and holiday life going on, laughing at some of the characters who came and went. They watched as two women in their thirties emerged from the door of the tea house, one of them clutching a tray of coffee and sandwiches. They both stood looking around for somewhere to sit. The dark-haired one spied Lyddy and Chris and started towards their table, her face lighting up. "Ah! Kindred spirits!" Her voice came across the tables with a strong American accent. She was attractive in a brash, loud way. Her large features went with her loud voice.

Lyddy and Chris waited for the two to reach their table and looked up at them. The American dumped her camera bag on the ground and pulled a spare chair out. "Can we join you, ladies?"

Lyddy glanced across at Chris and answered, "Yes, please do."

The fair-haired one stood holding the tray. "Are you sure? We always seem to be gate-crashing." She was English, softly spoken. She was the same height as her companion but looked like she'd just stepped out of the beach pages of a fashion magazine: slim, sun-tanned, her long hair bleached by the sun.

Chris smiled at her. "There's nowhere else to sit."

"Thank you." She put the tray on the table. The American sat down, pushed her sunglasses up to rest in her thick short hair and put on an English accent, "Are you going to be Mummy, darling?" She beamed across at Lyddy and Chris as her friend poured coffee from the pot.

Lyddy smiled back at her. "Kindred spirits?"

The American stared at her, her eyes crinkled in amusement. "We saw you on the beach yesterday."

Lyddy looked blank and glanced at Chris who was looking towards the harbour, a silly look on her face. She was obviously in on it but wasn't going to help out. Lyddy looked back to the American, slightly bemused, feeling rather slow on the uptake.

"Rose!" the fair one warned as she pushed her hair back over her shoulders and passed a cup of coffee and a plate of sandwiches along the table.

Rose, the American, leant forward, her eyes fairly twinkling. She lowered her voice almost conspiratorially in response to her companion's warning as she spoke to Lyddy, "It was something to do with the way you were accosting her back with your lips." She nodded her head towards Chris and smiled broadly at Lyddy. "When you thought no one was looking," she added. She tossed her head back and let out a delighted laugh at Lyddy's expression.

Lyddy looked at Chris who was grinning back at her. Bloody hell, she thought. How thick! She looked from the American to the English woman and back. Kindred spirits. She blushed through her suntan for the first time for as long as she could remember and grinned as well, rather stupidly. "Oh, I see."

Chris laid her hand briefly on Lyddy's arm as she spoke to the other two. "She'll recover in a minute," she told them. "It's usually Lyddy who has the upper hand on these things. I'm Chris, by the way. The slow one here is Lyddy."

Lyddy groaned. "Oh, God! You're going to make the most of this, aren't you?"

Chris went on, "The two sitting on the wall are Lyddy's children, Nikki and Peter."

"I'm Tweedie," the English woman offered and gestured towards the other, "and the loud one here is Rose."

"Nice kids," said Rose. "Are they always so good?"

"Thank you," Lyddy said, "and no, they're not, but they have their moments."

Nikki had noticed the conversation going on and slipped off the wall. She came over clutching the last of her cornet and worked her way in between Lyddy's legs to lean against her as she regarded the two strangers. Lyddy leant forward and slipped her arms around her. "Nikki, this is Tweedie and Rose."

"Hello." Nikki regarded them gravely.

"Hi," Rose said to her. "Great ice-cream here, don't you think?"

"It's Cornish."

"I know. It makes me fat, though." She patted her stomach.

"We've been fishing. On a boat," Nikki told her.

"Catch anything?"

"Yes, loads of mackerel," Nikki looked around and pointed at the bag lying by Lyddy's chair. "We're going to have them for tea."

"I wondered what that stink was."

Nikki warmed to her. "Are you a foreigner?"

Rose smiled widely at the childish impertinence. "Well spotted. I'm American."

Nikki smiled too. "I like foreigners." She looked at Tweedie and back to Rose. "I'll go and tell my brother. His name's Peter."

"Right," Rose said. "See you later."

Nikki went back to Peter and they sat heads together while she imparted her information to him. They heard a twang in her voice as she spoke. Lyddy laughed. "She'll have your accent off pat in five minutes."

"Tweedie," Chris said. "Where did you get the name Tweedie from?"

Rose patted her open mouth, pretending to yawn. "Oh, not that oft-told tale again."

Tweedie said placidly, "Shut up, Rose," and turned to Chris. "We moved when I was eleven and I only had one term to do in the new junior school. My mum didn't want to buy a new uniform just for one term so she made me wear this green tweed skirt and I got the nickname Tweedie." Then she added, "Actually, I prefer it to my proper name."

Rose finished for her, again affecting a yawn, "And I couldn't imagine being called anything else now."

"Oh, shut up, Rose," Tweedie told her again, good-humouredly. She looked at Chris and Lyddy, "Beware of repeating yourself in Rose's presence. She gets bored easily."

Chris and Lyddy were amused at the two of them. Lyddy asked, "What's your real name, Tweedie?"

"Annetta."

Rose said, "I could never have gone to bed with an Annetta."

"Ssh!" Tweedie glanced over at the children who were now engrossed in a conversation with a little boy in plastic sandals.

Lyddy laughed. "Annetta. It sounds like a food colouring."

Chris said, "Take no notice, Tweedie."

"Don't worry. I'm used to it."

Chris added, "Lyddy's had a bad day so far. She has some making up to do." Lyddy closed her eyes in resignation as Chris recounted the tale of the fishing trip.

"Oh, my God," Rose joined in. "Did you make loud, retching noises?"

"No, of course not. I never make loud retching noises when I'm sick. It just flowed out quietly."

Chris scoffed, about to contradict her.

"This is going down nicely with the sandwiches," Tweedie interrupted.

Rose guffawed. "Why is it that the English are never gathered together for more than five minutes before the conversation turns to toilets, bodies or sex?"

"That's because in your experience you're always there," Tweedie told her.

"No, it's not." Rose was convinced. "I've listened to other people's conversations and it's always the same."

"Well, that's indicative of the company you keep. Anyway, you were the one who brought up the subject of retching."

Chris took Lyddy's hand as she spoke, "That's not the only thing that's been brought up today."

Lyddy threw her a withering look, "Oh, hilarious."

Rose laughed again and leant forward, "And speaking of sex, how long have you two been together?"

"Since March," Lyddy said, glancing round to see if the conversation was being overheard; Rose had a loud voice.

"Newly weds! No wonder you look so pleased with yourselves." Rose was delighted. She went on, "Have you noticed that the divorce rate," she held up her fingers, scoring speech marks in the air, "is markedly lower among gay people?"

Tweedie interrupted, "Another of your social asides, dear. I'm beginning to think I should be keeping a note of these."

Rose wasn't put off. "Think about it," she told Lyddy and Chris. She lowered her voice now, obviously with an effort. "How many lesbians do you know, on a percentage basis, who split up after starting to live together? On a percentage basis, bearing in mind that the divorce rate for the country is supposed to be between thirty and forty per cent?"

Lyddy didn't point out that she and Chris weren't actually living together. She answered Rose, "Well, to be honest, you two are the only ones I've ever met, to my knowledge."

Rose rolled her eyes in an exaggerated gesture and stared at Lyddy. She leant forward and slapped Chris on the knee. "What's this, then? A cheese sandwich?" She put her hand theatrically on the table between them, palm down, and purred quietly, "Say after me. I am a lesbian."

Chris laughed and Lyddy held her hand over her eyes. "Yes, okay. You've made your point."

Tweedie said, "Rose, for God's sake!" She looked from Lyddy to Chris, "I apologise for my friend. She thinks she has a mission."

Rose blew her a kiss in return and bent down to unzip her camera bag. Pulling out a camera and screwing in a telephoto lens nearly a foot long, she stood up and slung the camera over her shoulder. She walked over to Nikki and Peter, holding out her hands to them, "Come on, you guys. Let's go and see what they've caught."

They turned to look in the direction of her gaze, and, seeing the fishing boat unloading its catch on the other side of the harbour, they both turned back to Lyddy. "Mum, can we go?" Nikki wriggled her bottom off the wall and took Rose's hand.

"Yes, alright. Don't go too near the edge." Lyddy altered her tone as she then spoke to Rose, to be sure of getting her attention, "Rose, don't let go of Nikki's hand within ten yards of the water. I guarantee she'll fall in if you do."

"Yeah, yeah," Rose muttered.

"Oh, Mum! You do fuss," Nikki said impatiently. Rose grabbed Peter's hand and started running with them across the road to the edge of the harbour wall. Sitting watching, they heard the sound of Rose's raised voice as she ran with them and the children's laughter.

Tweedie said to Lyddy, "Don't worry. She'll look after them." She gazed in the direction of Rose and the children, now walking together along the harbour wall. "Under that brash exterior is a heart of gold." She looked back to Lyddy, "And she loves children, believe it or not."

"How long have you been with Rose, Tweedie?" Chris asked.

"Nearly five years," Tweedie smiled. "It surprises me. It's gone so quickly. I was married for nearly five years before that and it seemed a life-time." She looked apologetic, "It was a bad marriage, that's all."

Lyddy liked her. She was quietly spoken, unassuming but sure of herself at the same time. "Mine was pretty grim, too," she said, her eyes watching the passage of Rose and the children around the edge of the harbour.

"But you have two lovely children from it."

"Yes," Lyddy smiled. "They're the good that came out of it."
Then she asked, "What about Rose?"

Tweedie grinned, "No, Rose has definitely never been married."

They sat talking, telling each other where they worked, where they lived. It turned out that Tweedie and Rose were staying in the flat above the post office in Port Isaac, a converted lifeboat house. It was a working holiday for Rose. She was a photographer, on an assignment for someone who was writing a book about Cornwall.

When Rose eventually returned with the children, they were both wearing baseball caps and colourful sunglasses. "Look what Rose buyed us," Nikki ran up to Chris to sit on her lap and slapped her old sunhat down on the table.

"Bought us," Lyddy told her. She watched as Rose and Peter came towards the table. "Thank you, Rose. That was kind of you." Peter perched himself on the arm of Chris's chair, leaning on her shoulder .

Rose beamed at her, "Holiday souvenirs. You can't go home without them."

"Rose is a photographer, Mum," Peter told her.

"So I hear."

"She let us look through her camera. We could see you sitting here from right across the harbour."

Rose patted her camera. "I took some pikkies of them. I'll send you the prints when I get them done."

Tweedie looked up at Rose, "Lyddy and Chris are staying in Port Isaac as well, Rose. They've invited us for a meal tomorrow night."

Rose groaned in anticipation. "Home cooked food. We've been eating restaurant nosh for three weeks."

Tweedie explained, "We haven't been very organised. We don't seem to get around to cooking."

Lyddy went into the tea rooms to get drinks for Nikki and Peter while Chris was explaining how to get to their house.

Lyddy took Chris's arm as they walked up the hill back to the car. "Well, what did you think?"

"Of Rose and Tweedie?"

"Mm."

"I like them. Rose is funny."

"Yes, so did I. Tweedie's her alter-ego. They're well matched, aren't they?"

"A bit like us, my darling." Chris looked at her.

"Oh, Chris. I'm never as loud as Rose. I'm not raunchy either."

"No, you're the English version. The English Rose."

"Very funny, you are on form today. Oh, God, they're vegetarians. What shall we cook them?"

"I don't know. We'll have to put our heads together. We'll think of something." Chris held up the bag of mackerel she was carrying, "I wonder if they eat fish."

"Definitely not curry," Lyddy said. "I'll bet Rose is not one to control her wind in company."

Chris laughed and squeezed Lyddy's arm. "I love you."

"Good. It makes me absurdly happy that you do."

"What, no cutting remark? No witty rejoinder?"

"Rejoinder! Good use of vocabulary for a mere infant's teacher. As if I would." Lyddy raised her voice to Nikki and Peter dawdling up the hill behind them, chattering, "Come on, you two. We'll have time for a scramble along the rocks before tea when we get back. The tide's not in till seven o'clock."

Chapter Sixteen

"Nikki, we're not playing polo, dear!" Annie called across the lawn. Nikki had just swung her croquet mallet in a wide arc to send her ball crashing into the bushes at the edge of the garden.

"But I'm miles behind everyone else," Nikki wailed.

"Go and get your ball, dear, and mind the petunias."

Nikki threw her mallet down and stomped across the lawn.

"Where does she get her sense of sportsmanship from?" Lyddy remarked dryly as she knocked her ball against Annie's.

"Well, she did get knocked off course a few times," Annie defended her.

"She hates losing, Annie, and you know it."

Lyddy placed her ball against Annie's, put her foot on it, and sent Annie's off away past the last hoop.

"Thank you, Lyddy." Annie walked away towards her ball. Lyddy stood still, lining her ball up to try to get through the last hoop and hit the peg in one.

"Mum! Don't hit mine!" Peter's ball was three feet away from the peg and just in Lyddy's line of fire.

"No chance," Bob called to him. He and Chris were leaning against the picnic table in the shade of the plane tree, chatting, watching the others.

"What do you bet?" Lyddy raised her voice to Bob.

"Mum!" Peter called again.

Lyddy aimed her ball onto the edge of the hoop. It passed through, deflecting off at an angle. She didn't want to knock Peter off – he was nearly home.

"Phew!" Peter gently knocked his ball, hitting the peg squarely. "Ha, ha. I'm home."

"Well done," Annie said, walking over. "Shall we finish now?" she asked Lyddy. "I think you're home next." She looked over at Nikki, who was standing at the edge of the lawn, waiting for her turn, her flushed face reflecting her disgust. "Do you want a swim, Nikki?" Annie called to her. "It's so warm."

"Don't we have to finish the game?" Nikki looked cheered at the offer.

"No, I think I've had enough, haven't you?" Annie was letting her off.

"Yes, I have." Nikki whacked her ball hard so that it shot across the lawn into the undergrowth the other side. "Stupid game."

"Nikki!" Lyddy felt obliged to check her. She loved the game when she was winning.

"Who's coming in with us?" Nikki asked, running over to Annie.

Bob pushed himself away from the picnic table. "I will. I won't swim – I'll come and watch you. Peter, are you coming?"

Peter walked with him up towards the house. "Yes, I want to try my flippers."

"Come on, Nikki," Bob put his hand out to her. "I can do the crossword. It's too warm out here for me."

Lyddy went over to Chris and sat on the edge of the table next to her, putting her arm through hers. Chris said, "You're a bit of a mean croquet player, aren't you?" She lowered her voice so that Annie wouldn't hear. "Where's the Pimm's? I thought it was mandatory to have a jug of Pimm's handy when you play croquet."

Lyddy smiled. "Yes, Annie's slipping, isn't she?" She raised her voice as Annie came towards them, "Do you want to get the lunch things cleared, Annie? Before we all collapse in the sun?" The picnic table was still covered in the debris from lunch which they'd had in the garden.

"Yes, we'd better." Annie waved her hands over the dirty plates. "Oh, these flies!"

"I'll help," Chris volunteered and turned to help Annie stack everything onto the trays.

"Leave the wine, Chris," Annie said. "We can have another glass when we've done this."

Lyddy put her mallet in the box and walked around the garden collecting the rest of the mallets and balls to put away. She went over to search for Nikki's ball in the bushes, found it, and tossed it in the box with the others. Then she went round pulling up the hoops. That done, she looked towards the picnic table and saw it was all cleared. She went over to pour herself some more wine and walked with it towards the sun-beds which had all been put out in a group together at the side of the garden. She sat on one of them, sipping her drink, thinking what wonderful weather they'd had so far for the school holidays. They had been back from Cornwall for two weeks and hadn't had a cloudy day in that time.

She put her glass down by the side of her and lay against the back rest. She thought how glorious the holidays were turning out to be, happy days and happy nights. Chris was virtually living at Lyddy's now; there had seemed little point in doing otherwise. She was part of the household now, part of the family. On the one occasion that she had stayed away, when her parents came to visit, the children had missed her and asked why she wasn't there.

The days seemed to be filling themselves up, as holidays do: picnics, days in the garden, outings to swimming pools, parks, adventure playgrounds, and the evenings by themselves. The week after they got back from Cornwall, they had gone to stay with Lyddy's father again. Lyddy smiled at the memory. An old friend of her father's came over one evening while they were there. They all hit the port and got very drunk, playing Scrabble, all four of them in fits of giggles at her dad's jokes and worsening quips at Lyddy and Chris's expense. Lyddy spent most of the next day under a tree in the garden while her dad and Chris played with the children and took them down to the river. They could handle their drink and wake up the next morning without trace of it. Lyddy ruefully remembered her hangover.

Chris's friend, Maggie, had come to stay at Lyddy's for two nights, sleeping on an air bed in the spare room. Laura, Maggie's seven year old, a bright tomboy, delighted in Peter and Nikki's make-believe games. It was chaos with them all in the house but Lyddy didn't think she had ever laughed so much. She and Maggie shared a similar sense of humour. Maggie and Chris were very close, almost like sisters.

Lyddy picked her glass up to take another sip, then rested her head back again. Chris's parents' visit hadn't been very successful. Lyddy had kept away again. Chris's mother had, in a roundabout way, broached the subject of Lyddy. At the meal table she said regretfully, quietly, "I had hoped to have grandchildren, Chris." Chris was their only child. Her father had sat, eating, with a pained expression on his face. Chris wasn't sure whether his feelings were on account of herself or her mother.

Chris had just said, "I'm sorry, Mum," and suggested again that maybe they should meet Lyddy, but her mother shook her head and looked regretful. She had changed her attitude, Chris thought, from outraged indignation to sad submission.

Lyddy brushed a fly away from her face and settled herself more comfortably on the sun-bed. How quickly the time was passing. Chris's departure loomed ahead and Lyddy felt a pang of misery at the thought. She pushed it away. She knew she had to start preparing herself for it but she didn't seem to be able to deal with it very well. She would only let herself think a day at a time. She blanked her mind to these thoughts and lay still, closing her eyes. She heard the sound of Annie's voice as she and Chris approached the sun-beds. Lyddy kept her eyes closed, stayed in her comfortable position.

"She's gone to sleep!" Lyddy heard Annie exclaim. She heard Chris's chuckle and the creaks of the sun-beds as they both settled themselves on them. There was the sound of a bottle chinking on glasses and Annie's voice again, "Here you are, have some wine."

"Thanks," Chris said.

Annie went on, referring to Lyddy again, "I don't know how she does it. She always managed to get out of clearing the table when she was little." Lyddy struggled to keep her face composed in feigned sleep as she swallowed a grin.

Chris told Annie, "This is her forte, falling asleep in the sun after lunch. She developed it to a fine art on holiday."

Annie said, seriously now, "You two are very close, aren't you?"

"Yes, we are."

"I've never seen Lyddy like this before," Annie remarked. There was a pause. "Never." They were keeping their voices low so as not to disturb her.

"Annie, *I've* never been like this before," Chris told her. Lyddy felt a surge of contentment but still didn't move, still kept her eyes closed.

It was quiet for a few moments; Annie had been thinking. "Chris, you know I was absolutely... shocked, I suppose," a pause again, "shocked, outraged, baffled even, when you and Lyddy first... well... got together."

"Yes, I know," Chris's voice was deliberately kind, not to make Annie feel uncomfortable.

"I couldn't understand, you see. Well, I suppose in a way I still don't understand," Annie went on. It struck Lyddy that for all her social awareness and decorum, Annie was honest, always honest. She continued, "But I do accept it now, you know. I don't know how it came about really." Lyddy heard Annie utter a short laugh. "I surprised myself. I think it was when I saw how happy you were, how happy Lyddy was. And, well, you do conduct yourselves with appropriate decency. In company, I mean. Oh, dear, that sounds patronising, doesn't it. Well, I suppose it is, isn't it?"

There was humour in Chris's voice as she answered, "Don't worry, Annie. I know what you mean."

Annie lowered her voice a bit more, a rare trace of wry amusement in her tone, confiding in Chris, "Good job Lyddy didn't hear me say that. I would have had to bear the brunt of her caustic wit, I suppose."

Chris giggled. "Yes, she does have a flair for capitalising on your weak moments. I'm the one who usually suffers in that respect." Lyddy mentally bit her tongue, enjoying this.

"Yes, well, you're so..." Annie was searching for the word, "so genuine, aren't you?" She wasn't patronising Chris now. Lyddy knew she meant what she said. She obviously thought highly of her to be talking to her in this way. She no longer made any pretence of her liking of Chris. Annie carried on, affectionately, sisterly, "Lyddy, now, Lyddy holds back. She doesn't always air her feelings openly. You have to read between the lines, sometimes. I suppose you're learning that, though."

"I am, indeed," Chris said. "You have to prod her a bit, don't you?"

Annie laughed. "Metaphorically. A good elbow in the ribs at times." Lyddy couldn't believe their conversation. She was having great difficulty in keeping a straight face. She wondered whether to open her eyes and come clean. There was a natural pause as she heard a glass touch the garden table beside the sun-beds and a creak of the springs. Annie said, chattily, "I suppose you're starting to get everything sorted out, aren't you? For your move, I mean. How long is it now?"

"Two weeks," Chris uttered quietly. Oh, Annie, get off this; say something else, Lyddy urged silently. This isn't allowed – it's taboo.

"Are you looking forward to it?"

There was a pause. Lyddy imagined Chris's expression. She heard the sadness in her answer. "I have very mixed feelings, Annie. I'm looking forward to starting the new job." Silence for a moment. "I can't pretend I'm looking forward to moving away."

"Oh, I think once you're up there, it won't be so bad," Annie told her, "Once you're in your new home and settled into your job."

Chris continued, as though Annie hadn't spoken, "In fact, to be honest, I'm dreading moving away. As each day goes by, I feel I'm on a countdown." Lyddy held her breath, wondering where this was going.

Annie didn't speak for a few moments, probably taking this in. Then she asked, "What does Lyddy say? How does she feel?"

"Annie, we don't talk about it." It was a bleak statement. Lyddy winced.

"No," Annie said, then her loyalty to Lyddy obviously got the better of her, unless she just wanted to cheer Chris up, allay her fears. She said, "Well, that's probably a good thing, isn't it? Not to make too much of it. I really think it won't be so bad. Oxford's not so far away, is it?"

Chris didn't answer. Lyddy didn't like to think what was going through her mind. Change the subject, Annie.

She did, with amazing deftness. "Will and Carl are away at the moment, aren't they? When do they come back?"

Chris allowed the conversation to veer away. "They're back this week. We had a card from them."

Annie started to tell Chris how fond she had grown of Will over the years, how good he had been to Lyddy on occasions, how he had helped her through some bad times. Lyddy relaxed; the danger was over. Then she pricked her ears up again. Annie was saying, continuing her train of thought, "Of course, for all Lyddy's armoury that she carries about her, she is liable to fall apart in an emergency."

"What!" Lyddy spluttered and an involuntary laugh escaped her throat. She opened her eyes and turned her head in the direction of Annie and Chris, only feet away from her. They were staring at her in surprise. Lyddy grinned sheepishly.

"How long have you been awake?" Annie demanded.

"Well, um..."

Chris was amazed. "Have you been awake all this time?" She saw Lyddy's expression. "You have! Lying there listening!"

Lyddy decided to fend them off by going on the attack. "Annie! What do you mean, I fall apart in an emergency?" She was highly amused.

"Really, Lydia!" Annie was quite out of sorts. "How could you? You've been listening. Eaves-dropping. Very sly of you." She sniffed. "I never know what to expect of you next."

Lyddy chortled. "Annie, don't be so pompous."

"Well, really!"

"What did you mean by that defamatory statement? I do not fall apart in emergencies."

Poor Annie. She knew that tone in Lyddy's voice and knew that whatever answer she gave would be shot down in flames. She was quite miffed and struggled to maintain some dignity. She pointedly ignored Lyddy and turned to Chris. "I think I'll go and find some towels. The children will be out of the pool soon. Would you like some coffee?"

Chris managed to keep a straight face. "Yes, thank you, Annie. Shall I come and help?"

Annie stood up. "No, thank you, I'll manage." With a withering glance at Lyddy, she sniffed again and went off towards the house. They heard the words "...quite intolerable, sometimes," muttered as she went. Lyddy and Chris looked at each other, stifling their laughter until Annie was well out of hearing.

"Lyddy," Chris chided her, her tone affecting gravity, "how could you? Poor Annie." Then her expression became more serious. "You heard the whole conversation?" she asked pointedly.

Lyddy caught her meaning, the bit about the impending move. She reached across and took Chris's hand, "I did." Chris stayed silent but searched her face for her reaction. Lyddy pressed her lips together, looking at Chris. She couldn't offer any consolation, for herself or for Chris. She didn't want to get into this, couldn't face it. "I don't want to think about it. Not now." She half expected Chris to say, 'Well, when?' but she didn't. Her face took on a look of resignation, accepting Lyddy's reluctance.

Lyddy sought to change the subject and cheer her up, "Um... if you were willing to risk bearing the brunt of my caustic wit, you might inform me how I, what was it, 'capitalise on your weak moments'." She finished this in a light, dry tone.

It worked. "Well, if you must listen to other people's conversations," Chris responded.

"I couldn't help it. It was so interesting. All about me."

Chris's mouth started to turn up at the corners. "You are so vain," she said, deadpan.

Lyddy wasn't put off. "Do you two have many of these little tête-à-têtes?" she asked. "Presumably, most of them are when I happen not to be within earshot. Very careless of you today."

"Lyddy, shut up."

"Oh, charming."

Chris laughed now. "I don't know why I love you. What on earth do I see in you?"

Lyddy started, "Well, it could only be my fine mind, highly tuned body, or..." She didn't get any further. Chris grabbed the cushion from Annie's sun-bed and hit her with it. Lyddy caught the cushion and put it behind her head.

Chris stood up and held out her hand, pulling Lyddy to her feet, and linked arms with her. "You're incorrigible," she said. "And don't eavesdrop on me, ever again," she added as they walked in the direction of the doors into the swimming pool.

Lyddy answered in a purring, conciliatory tone, "No, my darling."

"And apologise to Annie." Chris looked at her as she spoke. "Properly!"

"Yes, my love. Anything else?"

"Just one more thing. Are you listening?"

"Yes, my love."

"Stop being facetious. If you're nice to Annie for the rest of day, you can capitalise on my weakness when we get home tonight."

"Thank you, my darling. I look forward to it." Lyddy rested her head on Chris's shoulder and kissed her lightly on the neck. "Whoops! There's Annie. I shall start right now." She let go of Chris and walked towards the kitchen door as Annie was emerging with a tray of coffee cups. "Let me help, Annie darling!" she called cheerfully.

Chapter Seventeen

It was one of those sultry, late summer days, early September, the heat hanging in the air, no breeze, the smell of the garden heavy in the warmth. Lyddy took off her sunglasses, rubbed her eyes, put them back on and bent down. She had just finished cutting the grass and was cleaning the mower before putting it away. She glanced at her watch as she scraped the grass from the blades. Peter was at a friend's for the morning and she had to go and pick him up in twenty minutes. She looked up at Nikki playing with her rabbit on the grass, making a nest out of handfuls of newly-cut grass. She put the rabbit in the middle of the nest and he jumped out.

"Now, don't be naughty, Spit. Go to bed." Nikki went on to tell him what his punishment would be as she put him back on again.

Lyddy shut out the sound of Nikki's voice as she contemplated the knot in the upper part of her stomach. It was dread. She closed her eyes briefly, preparing herself for the afternoon. Chris was coming over after lunch and staying for tea. Lyddy grimaced, the Last Supper. She was moving the next morning, Friday, to her new house in Oxford. The schools started back on Tuesday and she had to go in on Monday. She needed the weekend to get settled into the house, to get organised.

They had largely continued to avoid the subject, not allowing it to surface to mar the last days of the holiday. They had kept busy: a day trip down to Studland beach; a picnic out with Jane and her children. Lyddy had taken Peter and Nikki into town to get them kitted out for the new term. Peter started his new school on Tuesday and had needed a new uniform. They had made things as happy as possible. But, Lyddy thought, there had been a desperation in them sometimes when they were alone together, unspoken of, but there. They had clung to each other on occasion, even Lyddy had been unable to lighten their feelings with her normal quips and teasing.

Oh God! she thought, you'd think she was moving to Australia. It was only Oxford, only eighty miles away, an hour and a half on a good day.

The knot was still in her stomach. I must shake myself out of this. This is ridiculous. She had to find some resolve.

Will and Carl had arrived back from their long overdue holiday the week before, suntanned, rested, full of it. They brought presents with them: a lovely translucent, white statuette of a naked woman for Chris, to take with her to Oxford. They gave Lyddy a small painting by an unknown Italian artist of two women, both naked, lying together on a rug by an open fire. Their accompanying comments had been suitable, of course, but little did they know, Lyddy thought. They didn't know of Chris's lovely wood fire, as far as she knew, not the significance of it, certainly.

Rose had paid them a flying visit whilst down their way on a job. She had stayed for lunch and made them promise to visit her and Tweedie in their flat in Croydon as soon as they could. She had been true to her word and brought the photos she had taken of Peter and Nikki in Padstow. There was also one of Lyddy and Chris taken on the beach one day which they hadn't even known she had taken. It was a close-up, taken as Lyddy leant her head on Chris's shoulder, speaking into her ear. Rose was obviously talented. It had captured their mood precisely, Lyddy smiling happily as she spoke and Chris laughing in response. It now sat, framed, on the dresser in the kitchen.

Lyddy glanced up to see what Nikki was doing, aware that she could no longer hear her voice. She was standing up on the swing, bending her knees, trying to get going. Dodger was sprawled on his side on the lawn in the sun, the rabbit crouched between his legs.

Lyddy brushed the remaining grass off the mower, wondering how she was going to cope. Chris would be over in an hour and she felt totally inadequate for what was to come and totally miserable. She heard footsteps on the gravel path at the side of the house and her heart missed a beat.

"Hello! Anyone home?" It was Annie's voice.

The latch on the gate clicked and Annie appeared, clutching a pot of lilies planted in a large, beautifully decorated pot. She held it out. "It's 1880's. Don't you think it's beautiful. I planted them myself," she said, looking at the lilies. "Just a little present for Chris to take with her." She looked around, "Is she here?"

Lyddy stood up and took a deep breath, "Annie, it's lovely." She kissed Annie on the cheek. "Chris will be really pleased." She tried to keep her tone normal.

She took the pot from Annie and started towards the kitchen. "Come in for a minute. I've got to go and fetch Peter soon."

"Oh, I'm not stopping. I just wanted to say good luck and see you soon." Annie followed Lyddy into the kitchen and then focused on her face in the relative dimness. "What?"

Lyddy's eyes were brimming with tears. She had taken her sunglasses off.

Annie understood. "Oh, Lyddy!" She took a step forward and put her arms round her. Lyddy let her tears come, knowing that she would handle the afternoon better if she released some of the emotion now.

Annie did her best, "She's only going to Oxford, Lyddy. It's not the end of the world," her tone kind. She added, "There'll be other holidays, weekends, Christmas, half terms." She took Lyddy's shoulders in her hands and pushed her away to look at her, "You'll see each other quite a lot, still."

Lyddy controlled her tears, searching for a handkerchief. Annie passed her one.

"It's not the same though, is it? Oh, Annie, I'm going to miss her. And," Lyddy blew her nose, "I've got to get through this afternoon." She gave a bleak smile, "I'm supposed to be the 'strong' one."

"Oh, dear. I had no idea you felt like this." Annie was truly upset. "I didn't think. Oh, Lyddy, I hate to see you like this. You've been so happy, haven't you? The children adore her, don't they?"

Annie was saying all the wrong things and the tears came again. Lyddy sat down at the table, clutching the handkerchief as she leant her forehead on her hand.

"Can I do anything? Would you like me to stay?"

Lyddy got herself under control. "No, Annie. Thank you." She smiled another weak smile, "I'm just trying to summon some courage. I'll be alright."

She wiped her eyes and blew her nose again. She got up to look in the mirror above the fridge. "I think I'd better put my sunglasses back on. I've got to go and get Peter." She looked back at Annie's anxious face, "I'm alright, really. I'm okay now." She picked up her car keys and sunglasses. "Come on, I'll walk out with you." She glanced again at the plant on the table, "And thank you for the present, it was really nice of you."

"That's alright. It's from both of us, with our love."

Lyddy pecked her cheek as she walked to the door, "Thanks, Annie."

She called Nikki to come and get in the car and they walked round to the front of the house.

"Where is Chris, anyway? I thought she'd be here," Annie asked.

"She's spent the morning at home, sorting out her papers and getting the place cleaned up."

"Has she packed everything?"

"No, the removal men are doing it all."

"Oh, well. That's saved some time, then."

"Yes."

"Give me a ring if you need me, won't you?"

"I will. Thanks, Annie."

"Say good luck to Chris for me."

"I will."

At tea time, the children chattered away. Peter was talking about his new school, whether they would play football, Nikki talking about her new teacher, which reader she would be on. Lyddy made no attempt to join the conversation except to answer the occasional question from them. Chris was quietly picking at her food, speaking when spoken to.

They had taken the children out for the afternoon, to get out of the house. They took Dodger for a walk in some woods where it was cooler and Lyddy and Chris had strolled arm-in-arm while the children looked for suitable trees to climb.

"Did you get everything done?" Lyddy had asked.

"Yes, I even wrapped the Naked Lady," Will's present, "in case she gets broken."

They were both very subdued, walking without speaking, holding each other's arms.

Now, at the table, Peter was asking Chris about her new house, "Has it got a garden?"

Chris looked up, "Yes, a big one. There's an apple tree; it would be perfect for a tree house."

She was making an effort, Lyddy thought, though her voice was quiet. Nikki and Peter asked more questions, about the bedrooms, how big it was.

Then Nikki asked, "Do you have to move, Chris?"

Chris looked again from her half-finished meal, her face set, a desolate look in her dark eyes. "Yes, I do, sweetie."

"Why can't you stay here?"

"Because I have a new job to go to." Chris's expression was bleak. She was struggling to hold back her tears.

"Why can't you come back to my school? Mrs Carlisle wouldn't mind."

"I can't. A new teacher is starting at your school next week. Instead of me."

Nikki thought about this, her face solemn. "I don't want you to move. I'll miss you. Won't you, Mum?"

"Yes, I will, darling," Lyddy answered quietly.

Chris couldn't stand it. She pushed the rest of her food to one side of her plate and stood up. Lyddy's heart sank. She saw Chris's eyes filling with tears as she walked over to the sink. She started running the hot tap to wash up, something to do.

"Will we still see you?" Peter asked, his face grave too.

Lyddy looked over at Chris's back. Chris put the back of her hand to her mouth and shook her head. She couldn't trust herself to speak.

Lyddy pressed her lips together, summoning a steady voice, and said, "Yes, of course we will." Peter looked at her and Lyddy went on, "We'll go and see Chris at her new house and she'll come and visit us at weekends." She smiled bravely at Nikki and Peter, their faces serious, taking this in. Peter watched Chris at the sink.

"Why don't you two go and see to Twitch and Spit?" Lyddy suggested. "You haven't fed them today. Their food's outside in the bowl."

"We haven't had pudding yet, Mum," Nikki pointed out.

Peter grabbed Nikki's hand, "Come on. I don't want pudding anyway."

"I do."

"Nikki, Come *on*!" he pulled her hand. Nikki got the message. They got down from the table and went out into the garden, Peter shutting the door behind them.

Lyddy stood up and went over to Chris. She turned as Lyddy put her arms round her and pushed her face into Lyddy's shoulder, her sobs making her body heave. Lyddy squeezed her tightly and rubbed her cheek in Chris's hair. She swallowed the lump in her throat and it came back. This had been brewing for a while, particularly this week; this was what she had been dreading. She was determined not to break as well. The removal men were coming at eight in the morning so Chris was going back home tonight. Lyddy would let her tears come again then.

She moved her arms to hold Chris against her as closely as possible and closed her eyes, waiting. After a while, Chris wasn't heaving so much, her sobs quieter. She took a breath between them and said into Lyddy's shoulder, "I knew this would happen." She tried to control her breathing to speak.

"I know," Lyddy said gently. "So did I."

Chris took another deep breath, "You're so strong, aren't you?" Her voice was muffled against Lyddy's T-shirt.

"One of us has to be."

"Old joke," she managed, "and poor taste."

"I know." Lyddy pressed her cheek against Chris's, feeling the wetness of her tears.

"It hurts. I love you so much."

"I know," Lyddy breathed the words.

"I'm finding this really hard."

"I know."

Chris attempted humour, "Is that all you can say?"

"Okay." Lyddy lifted Chris's head to look at her, "Okay?" She wiped Chris's cheeks with her fingers, reached for a tissue from her pocket and held it against Chris's nose, like a child, "Blow!" Chris blew into it and laughed through her tears.

She put her head back on Lyddy's shoulder and hugged her tightly. "I don't think I can bear this. I'm going to miss you so much."

"So am I." They held on to each other. Lyddy found the resolve she had been searching for all day, "The first week will fly by. Before you know it we'll be tumbling in through the door, creating havoc, making too much noise."

"Yes," Chris said into Lyddy's neck, "and come Sunday night, all I'll have left of you will be the biscuit crumbs in the bed."

"Oh, Chris, don't. You're making this even harder, for both of us."

"I know."

Lyddy looked at her, met her eyes for several moments. "I love you," she said simply, with feeling.

"You're not being serious for once, are you?" Chris smiled tearfully. "Goodness, it might all be worth it, after all!"

Lyddy made a face, "Ha! Ha!"

"I thought that was my line."

"Good. You're cheering up." Lyddy hugged her again then held Chris's face in her hands. "Help me do the washing up and we'll get the children to bed. Then I'll really cheer you up."

Chris grinned this time, her face still wet, "I doubt it. Give me a clue."

"No," Lyddy said. "Use your imagination," and kissed her on the lips. She pushed the button on the cassette player. 'Brown Eyed Girl' burst forth, Van Morrison, "That's better," and she started piling up the plates on the table, joining in the song in full voice.

Chris turned back to the sink, red-eyed but smiling.

When Chris finally left, they clung to each other at the front door. She eventually disentangled herself, bent down to pick up the plant from Annie and looked at Lyddy for several seconds, her eyes echoing her misery. Lyddy's face was set as she looked back. She couldn't even raise a parting smile. Chris stepped outside and walked to her car without speaking. Lyddy stood in the doorway as she drove away.

Chapter Eighteen

They arrived at Chris's just after ten the next Saturday morning, having got up early. Lyddy felt it was too much for the children to pile in the car straight after school, to face what would be a two hour drive in rush hour traffic on a Friday afternoon.

They found the road after going round in circles for a while: a wide, tree-lined avenue with double-fronted houses set back, 1920's probably. Lyddy drove the car into number ten's drive. Chris's car was parked in the wide, open garage at the side of the house. The drive curved round the small lawn of the front garden and exited out through the other end of the tall hedge bordering the lawn. She stopped the car in front of the house.

"Wow! Nice house, Mum," Peter said as he climbed out.

"It's enormous!" said Nikki. Not enormous, but it was bigger than Lyddy had imagined.

The front door opened as Lyddy closed the car door behind her. Chris stood at the top of the steps, smiling. She came down to meet Nikki and Peter who ran towards her, throwing their arms round her waist at the same time. She hugged their shoulders, one arm each and bent to kiss their proffered lips. "Hello, my lovelies."

"I thought we'd never get here," Peter told her. "Mum got lost."

"I didn't get lost," Lyddy laughed as she came up behind them. "We saw a bit of Oxford on the way."

"Yes, you did," Nikki insisted, still with her arms round Chris. "You said we were lost." She looked up at Chris, "Can we look round the house?"

"Yes, of course you can. Your bedroom's the one next to the bathroom." Chris hugged Nikki again before she dashed into the house after Peter.

She straightened up to Lyddy who was waiting, smiling, and they put their arms round each other. "Hello, my darling." They stood wordlessly for several moments, cheeks together, eyes closed, absorbed in the physical contact.

"Come on," Chris moved first, taking Lyddy's hand. "We'll start the neighbours talking. I'll make you a coffee and show you round."

The sun streamed in through the open front door. Chris led Lyddy through the hallway to the kitchen at the back, Lyddy glancing in through the open doorways. A wide staircase led off to the right at the end of the hall by the kitchen door. The kitchen was big enough for a table and chairs in the middle. A big archway opened onto a breakfast room, obviously the wall had been knocked down between the two at some time. "Gosh, it is big," Lyddy commented. "You must rattle around here after your cottage."

Chris smiled as she filled the kettle, "I do a bit. It's a very friendly house, though. I don't feel it's overbearing." She glanced over at Lyddy as she added, "I rattle around anywhere now without you." She put the kettle on and walked round the kitchen table to hug Lyddy again. "How has your week been, my darling?" she asked, touching her forehead to Lyddy's.

"Busy," Lyddy answered, "and lonely."

"Yes, I know. That sums mine up, too."

They started to kiss and heard the children's footsteps coming down the stairs. Drawing apart, Lyddy took Chris's arm.

"I want to hear all about school. Show me round first. This house is gorgeous."

They went round the house all together. The sitting room to the right of the front door was lovely, Lyddy thought, sun-filled, windows to the front and side, big open fireplace, marble surround. The children delighted in the window seats as they lifted up to reveal storage space inside. "Perfect for hide and seek," Nikki proclaimed. "Can we play, Mum?"

"Oh, Nikki, not now! We'll play later."

"Promise?"

"Promise."

The dining room to the other side of the front door was the same size, dominated by another fireplace, window seats again, an enormous dining suite filling the room. "I don't think I'll use this much," Chris commented.

Upstairs, Nikki and Peter showed Lyddy into their bedroom at the back of the house. Lyddy looked into the second bedroom at the front. Curtains half drawn, it was filled to the brim with furniture and boxes. The bed had been stood on its side against the wall.

"Goodness! Is this all yours?" she asked Chris.

"Yes, Mrs Everton cleared the room out for me. I won't need my stuff while I'm here."

They went into the sun-filled main bedroom, leading off at the top of the stairs. Solid wood built-in wardrobes stretched from behind the door along the length of the wall to the window at the front.

"What an enormous bed," Lyddy said.

"That's what I said when I saw it," Chris smiled. "Apparently, Mrs Everton's husband had arthritis and she said it stopped her getting nagged in the night for kicking him."

"Perfect," Lyddy smiled, still holding onto Chris's arm.

The children were trying the space under the window seat for fit. Lyddy added, "This is a lovely house. I'll be able to picture you now when I think about you." She squeezed Chris's arm with her own.

They had their coffee downstairs, the children had drinks and they got their bags from the car. Chris said that she hadn't had time to get any food in, so they went into Oxford to stock up.

When they got back they elected to have lunch in the garden. They all marvelled at its size. More or less square in shape, the lawn was dotted with well-established trees and shrubs. The large apple tree at the bottom was old, gnarled, misshapen; and perfect for a tree house, as Chris had said.

After lunch, Lyddy and Chris sprawled on sun-beds, the September sun very warm. Chris told Lyddy about her job, how her week had been. They had spoken on the phone during the week but they filled in the gaps of their news. Lyddy was pleased. Chris was enjoying the job, had been very busy and hadn't been home before six each evening. Lyddy told Chris about her new classes, about Peter starting his new school, how Nikki had got off to a bad start with the new teacher by knocking a pot of powder paint into the fish tank.

Chris laughed and took Lyddy's hand across the gap between the sun-beds. She took her sunglasses off to squint at Lyddy, "It's lovely to have you here. I've missed you so much."

Lyddy looked across at her, "It's lovely to be here. I'm not sure how I got through the week." She made a face, "It's very lonely in my bed."

Chris's face grew serious. "It's a good job I've been kept busy," she said. "Sometimes I ache for you."

"I know," Lyddy answered simply. Exactly how she felt.

They lay watching the children on the apple tree; it was perfect for climbing. Lyddy thought fleetingly of having to leave the next afternoon, such a short time away. She pushed the thought away, and said, seeing Nikki put her hand on a branch just within her reach, "If we're not dashing off to the hospital by the end of the day, I'll eat my sunglasses."

"Ready or not, I'm coming!" Nikki came out of the toilet, under the stairwell, the counting house. She had got her game of hide and seek. She went through the downstairs rooms, peering behind curtains, lifting up window seats, looking behind furniture, then went to the bottom of the stairs. "I'm coming up," she hollered again. "I know you're up there."

She found Peter and Chris both in the spare front bedroom. There was hardly any room to move in it. Peter was curled up in a half-filled box of books. Chris was squeezed in under the upturned sofa. Both the children tried to squeeze in with her and they all laughed and giggled as they tried to get out.

"Come on," said Chris, leading the way back across all the furniture. "Where's your mum?"

They went in the other rooms, checking under beds, behind curtains. Nikki pulled the drawers out of a chest.

"Don't be daft," Peter scoffed. "She wouldn't fit in there."

They checked the large airing cupboard in the bathroom, then stood on the landing, listening.

"Mum!" Peter yelled. "Where are you?"

A muffled laugh came from the big bedroom and the children dashed in there. They stood still in the room. "Mum!"

"I think I'm stuck," her laughing voice came from the long built-in wardrobe. They opened all the doors and didn't see her. Chris pulled a chair across and stood on it. She had wedged herself at the back of the shelf which ran the length of the cupboard above the hanging rail.

At the sight of Chris peering over, Lyddy pressed her face to the shelf, shaking in silent laughter.

"How did you get up there?" Chris asked.

The children stood on the bed so they could see. Lyddy looked down at them and shook her head, unable to speak. The game always affected her this way. She finally raised her head again, her eyes wet. "What took you so long?" she started laughing again. "I've been lying here listening to you opening cupboards, pulling out drawers." She couldn't control herself.

Nikki and Peter looked at Chris, putting feigned expressions on their faces. "Oh, my Gawd," Nikki said, "Mother's got the giggles."

Lyddy managed to say, "Don't say that, Nikki," before she was off again and she rolled over on the shelf, doubled up.

Peter was laughing too. It was infectious. He pulled Chris's hand, "Come on, let's leave her there. She'll calm down then."

"No!" Lyddy's face appeared at the edge of the shelf, they could see she was about to start again. "I don't think I can get down." She rested her face on her forearm and her uncontrollable mirth got to them all. Nikki and Peter rolled on the bed.

Chris eventually got her down by standing on the chair and letting Lyddy ease herself onto her shoulders. She managed to stay upright to take a step onto the floor and then leaned towards the big bed and they both fell on to it. The children took full advantage and leapt on them excitedly.

Lyddy, finally spent, managed to pull herself off the bed and stood looking at them, amusement still in her eyes. "That's it! No more hide and seek. I shall have a heart attack."

"Oh, Mum! We haven't all counted yet."

"Yes, we have. I'm done for."

Chris disentangled herself from their arms and legs and knelt up on the bed. "Shall we get some tea? I'm starving."

They all agreed and Nikki and Peter stayed on the bed, using it as a trampoline as Lyddy and Chris left the room.

"Don't go too mad. You'll break the bed," Lyddy threw back at them as she walked out. She and Chris put their arms round each other as they walked down the stairway.

Lyddy kissed Chris on the cheek as they went, "I love this house."

Chris grinned at her, "That's about the fourth time you've said that today."

"I know. You said it was nice, but it's beautiful. I wonder what Mrs Everton would think if she knew she'd got a house full of madcaps staying in it?"

"I don't think she'd mind, actually," Chris commented. "She's a lovely lady."

At the bottom of the stairs they turned into the kitchen and stood hugging each other. The sun now streamed in through the kitchen window. Lyddy breathed her words into Chris's ear, "I've missed you."

Chris drew her head back and leant her forehead on Lyddy's for a moment, then they kissed, the first chance they'd had since Lyddy arrived with the children. A long kiss, exploring each other's mouths, making up for the week they had spent apart. Finally they let it end and held their cheeks together.

"Oh, Lyddy!"

Lyddy heard the quiet anguish in Chris's voice. She wondered somewhat bleakly, as she stood with her head tucked into Chris's neck, how they were going to live like this. She gave Chris a squeeze, "Let's get something to eat."

They had their tea. The children had showers standing up in the bath and insisted on Chris reading to them before bed. They had brought their books and favourite toys in their suitcase. Then Chris said goodnight and left Lyddy to tuck them into bed.

Finally, Lyddy came downstairs to the kitchen. It was still light; it wouldn't be dark for another hour or so. She rested her bottom on the edge of the table. "That's what I need," she said, watching Chris load soap into the dishwasher and switch it on.

Chris came over to Lyddy and hugged her, unsmiling. "I know what I need," she said quietly.

Lyddy didn't even consider one of her usual facetious quips, not this time. "Do you know what I'd like to do?" she asked softly. "Get a large gin and tonic, fill that enormous bath and get in it with you."

"Okay."

They lay in the deep bath. Chris was sitting up, resting her back on the sloping end with Lyddy lying back between her drawn up legs. Chris had her arms round Lyddy's neck, gently massaging her body in the soft water, occasionally pushing a handful of water up over Lyddy's shoulders where the water didn't reach. Their drinks sat on the tiled surround, half finished.

Lyddy put her hands over Chris's. She felt very subdued, sad almost. She wondered again whether they would get used to this, but thought maybe it was early days and things would settle down. She had been so pleased to see Chris that morning, she could have cried.

Chris lifted her legs and wrapped them round Lyddy so that her feet rested between Lyddy's legs. She had barely spoken since they got in the bath. Now, she said, "Lyddy, this is going to be very hard. I can't help myself thinking about you having to go tomorrow."

Lyddy waited, trying to think of some consolation to offer. She couldn't.

Chris went on, "It's almost as if I missed you so much last week and I shall miss you so much again next week, that it's taking the pleasure out of being with you." She added, "I enjoyed today, but now it's hit me between the eyes again."

"I know," Lyddy said quietly. "I feel the same way." She didn't feel like putting on a brave face. She moved her hands up and down Chris's smooth thighs, then she said gently, "It'll get better, easier. It'll take time."

Neither of them spoke again for a while. Chris continued to rub her hands gently over Lyddy's body. She pressed her lips to Lyddy's head and held them there, "I love you so much," the words whispered into Lyddy's hair.

Lyddy moved her head so that she was looking up at Chris, at her tanned face, her short dark hair wet at the bottom from the water, her lovely cheekbones shaping the top of her cheeks, her dark eyes looking sadly back. She felt so right, complete, being with Chris and yet she felt so wretched. She was overwhelmed by the feeling. "Let's go to bed," she murmured.

Chris didn't answer. They stood up, got out of the bath and dried each other off. Lyddy shook her hair down and reached over the bath to pick up their glasses with one hand. They didn't bother to put anything on as they walked to the bedroom, arms around each other.

Lyddy and the children left at four the next afternoon. It had been a tiring weekend for them all. She didn't want to wait until after tea before leaving. It would be too late for the children with school the next day.

She sat in the driver's seat with the engine running, holding Chris's hand through the open window. Chris's eyes were wet.

Lyddy mouthed, "I love you," squeezed her hand one last time and let out the clutch. Chris stood in the driveway, watching as they stopped at the roadway to wait for a passing car. She just waved in reply to the children's farewell cries.

Chapter Nineteen

They decided, as a rule, that Chris would come and stay at Lyddy's rather than Lyddy and the children go to Oxford. They all loved being in the big house but it meant that they had less time together. When Chris came to Lyddy's, she left after school so that she had Friday evening there and she didn't leave till late on Sunday evening.

Lyddy spent one weekend by herself with Chris in Oxford. Annie offered to have Nikki and Peter for the weekend so they could 'have some time to themselves'. Lyddy was grateful. On the other weekends of the first half of the autumn term, Chris came to stay at Lyddy's.

The first Saturday morning of the half-term holiday, Lyddy was out in the garden. She had a sweater and jeans on; it wasn't warm, the sky overcast. She was cleaning out the rabbits' hutch. Nikki and Peter had gone to an agricultural show for the day with Jane's family. The had a seven-seater so they could all fit in one car. Lyddy hadn't gone with them, as Chris was arriving after lunch, to stay for the week. She had stayed in Oxford the night before. Mrs Everton was coming down from Suffolk that morning to collect some papers and other odds and ends. Chris thought she should stay and see her. Mrs Everton's mother was unlikely to care for herself again and she was going to move to Suffolk permanently to be with her. She was putting the house on the market. She was also going to an auctioneer's while she was in Oxford to arrange the sale of most of her furniture and other items in the house which she would no longer need. Chris would have to find somewhere else to live, but Mrs Everton had told her to take her time. The house wouldn't be sold in a day.

Lyddy leaned back on her heels, pushing cabbage stalks through the bars of the clean cage, the rabbits grabbing the ends and pulling them through. She felt happier than she had since term started at the prospect of Chris being here for a whole week. The last few weeks had been a strain, but she thought she was beginning to adjust to it. It would be like it had been in the summer. They were going to Will's that evening for a dinner party as it was Carl's birthday. Lyddy made a mental note to wrap his present later. They were all invited to Annie's for the day tomorrow.

She felt like a child waiting for Christmas while she passed the morning until Chris came. She was excited for Chris, too. After that first weekend, things had been a little easier for Lyddy. She had coped better with the short time they had together. She found it easier when Chris came down here. Chris was still finding it hard, not as bad as that first weekend, but there was a sadness in her sometimes, when they were alone together. There were always tears when it came to parting.

Lyddy thought ruefully that the relationship had changed subtly. It was inevitable, she supposed, that they weren't totally relaxed and able to be themselves in the circumstances. Last weekend, she thought back, Chris had been quiet. She said she thought she was coming down with flu; it was rife in school. When Lyddy spoke to her on the phone during the week, she hadn't yet succumbed but she hadn't been herself. Lyddy hoped she would be alright for the holiday. She was happy for Chris at the thought of a week together and thrilled for herself.

She heard a car pull up on the gravel drive and wondered who it might be, Annie, maybe. She kept an ear out for the door bell while she pushed the dirty straw into a carrier bag. If it was Annie, she would come round the side to the back door. Lyddy heard the car door slam and footsteps come down the gravel path at the side of the house. She stood up, tying the handles of the bag together as the latch went. Chris came through the gate and closed it behind her. Dodger ran up to her, wagging his tail. She took no notice of him.

Lyddy threw the carrier bag over towards the dustbin and stepped towards her, delighted. "Hello, my love! I wasn't expecting you till this afternoon! Did you see Mrs Everton?"

Chris turned from the gate towards Lyddy. Her face was pale against her navy sweatshirt, her lips set as she looked at Lyddy. She looked awful, as if she might pass out at any moment.

Lyddy put her arms out as she moved closer, "Oh, Chris! Are you alright?"

Chris stood still, looking at Lyddy, her face ashen. She said quietly, "Lyddy, I have to talk to you."

Lyddy wondered what on earth could have happened. She had never seen Chris like this, not even on that awful day before she moved. She briefly wondered whether it was something to do with her parents. She took Chris's arm and led her towards the kitchen door, "Come in, my darling. What's happened? You look terrible."

Chris didn't answer. She allowed Lyddy to lead her into the kitchen and gently took her arm away. She went to the other side of the table and sat down. She leant her forearms on the kitchen table, clasped her hands together, stared at the table for a moment and then raised her eyes to look at Lyddy. Her mouth was still set, her lips still slightly pressed together, her lovely features tense and strained. Lyddy watched anxiously and waited for her to speak.

Chris took a deep breath, her dark eyes stricken in her gaze. "Lyddy," her voice was unsteady. She swallowed and controlled it after a pause. "Lyddy, I can't live like this."

Lyddy stared at her, not comprehending.

"Lyddy," Chris took another deep breath, "it's destroying me. I can't handle being apart from you." She looked down at the table again. "I love you so much it hurts when I leave you, a real pain in my chest. You can't imagine how empty I feel when you drive away from the house; I feel like half a person. I hate," she paused in reflection, "I *hate* leaving you to drive back from here on a Sunday night to an empty house."

Lyddy was unable to reply. She stared at Chris, waiting for her to continue, aware of an awful feeling of foreboding.

Chris went on, "I throw myself into work during the days but I go around in the evenings with this ache inside me. Even the weekends I can't really enjoy because I know it's so short and before I know it you will be gone or I will be back in the car to face another week up there without you."

She now looked up at Lyddy again, desperately trying to control her emotions. "Lyddy, I've never loved anyone as I love you, never even come close. I didn't know you could love someone like this. I know you love me too, just as much, but you're stronger. You can be rational. You've said it yourself; you can put things away in your head, deal with them. I can't. I'm so unhappy I can hardly think sometimes. I want to be with you, have fun with you, live my life with you." She took another deep breath, still gazing at Lyddy as she spoke, "It's not possible like this. I just can't handle it. It's no way to live. I feel I'm only half alive."

Lyddy couldn't take this in. She didn't really understand but felt only dread. She said, quietly, "What are you saying? Exactly?"

"We have to finish this. Call it off." Chris saw Lyddy's expression and dropped her gaze, pushing on, "I'm so sorry. I would rather learn to live without you than carry on in this misery. If I stayed here this week, I would just be thinking about having to leave again at the end of it." She raised her eyes to Lyddy again as she added, "You only have one life. I just can't live mine like this."

Lyddy had leaned back to the kitchen worktop and was holding the edge of it with her arms outstretched, hands to either side, her face echoing her shock. Chris couldn't cope with Lyddy's look. She stood up.

"Chris, can we talk about this?" Lyddy managed to say, dimly aware that Chris might walk out of the door at any moment. She added quietly, "You've just thrown this on me. I can hardly even take it in, let alone think about it. Can we *talk* about it?" She stopped for a moment. "Bloody hell! I can't imagine life without you now and you're standing there saying *'call it off'*?" Her turmoil and desperation were coming out in anger.

Chris pushed her lips together, holding back tears which threatened. She went to the back door, paused there, then reached out a hand to lay it briefly on Lyddy's arm. She managed to say, "I can't, Lyddy. I'm sorry. I can't live that way." Her breath caught in a sob, "I love you too much."

Lyddy didn't even try to stop her, aware that it wouldn't have any effect. She remained where she was, hands still clasping the edge of the worktop behind her. She heard the latch go, the gate close, footsteps on the gravel, the car door slam, engine start and then Chris was gone.

"Oh, my God!" she murmured, unable to move, unable to think. Her world had just been turned upside down; she didn't know which way was up. She just stood still. She stood there for maybe five minutes, her mind in a whirl, her eyes moving absently round the kitchen.

Eventually, she walked over to the phone on the wall and picked it up, dialled a number. A voice spoke at the other end.

"Carl?" Lyddy said. She pulled a chair over to sit down.

"Lyddy? Hello, my love. Are you still coming tonight?"

"Carl."

"What is it, love? What's wrong?" His voice was gentle.

"Is Will there?" she managed to whisper, her voice about to break.

"I'll get him."

Will's voice came over the line, "Lyddy?" His concern showed in his voice.

Lyddy broke, "Will!" It was a wretched cry.

"Oh, Christ. I'll be there in fifteen minutes." The line went dead.

Lyddy put the phone down on the table, leant forward and cried into her arms crossed on the table in front of her.

By the time Will arrived, she had herself more in control, still sitting in the same chair, her face wet, her eyes red, gazing unseeing as she thought about what had just happened. Will came through the side gate and straight through the door into the kitchen, ignoring Dodger fussing around his legs.

The sight of him, his concerned face, his arms outstretched, set her off again. She pushed the chair back with her legs as she stood up to fall into Will's arms and sobbed inconsolably into his sweater. He put his arms round her and waited patiently, his head bent, resting on top of hers.

Half an hour later, she was halfway through her second brandy and they were in the sitting room. They sat on the sofa, Lyddy slumped into the back cushions, Will perched on the edge, next to her, at an angle so that he was almost facing her.

Lyddy's tears were spent, her emotions drained. She stared at the floor and forced a small laugh, though it was only a sound. "You're going to tell me you told me so."

"No, I'm not," he said gently. Whether he thought it or not, he wasn't letting on.

"I suppose I should have seen this coming," Lyddy said quietly. She took a gulp of her brandy. "Typical me. Put it away in the back of your head if you can't deal with it."

"Don't be silly."

She looked up, took another swig from her glass. "That's what I've done, Will. I can look back now and that's what I've done. I should have seen this coming."

She thought of Chris's attitude to the separation, right back to when she was first offered the new job; the journey back from her dad's after Easter; the various times it was mentioned and how bleakly Chris had anticipated them being apart. She thought of the day before she moved and the first weekend Lyddy stayed in Oxford and all the other weekends. All the signs were there. Lyddy had always been at pains to make light of it or side-step the issue.

She realised now that she hadn't allowed herself to face the fact that Chris had slowly become more unhappy, more morose. She thought of what a happy, care-free person she was at heart, how all this had affected her. Lyddy mentally kicked herself.

"Well," said Will. "What could you have done?"

"Oh, Will. I could have faced it. I could have made myself sit down and face the situation. Made myself think how I would feel if we parted. I know the answer to that, don't I? And I could have asked myself what could be done about it. There is a situation here which is unendurable. How can it be changed?"

"You were the one who persuaded Chris to go ahead with the new job," Will told her gently.

Lyddy looked up in surprise for him to explain.

"She told me," he grinned apologetically. "We had a talk one day, out in the kitchen at the flat. You and Carl were in the lounge arguing about education."

Lyddy vaguely remembered, after Will and Carl had returned from their holiday. "What did she tell you?"

Will thought for a moment. "That she had been reluctant to take the job but you'd been so persuasive. You made her feel she would be failing herself if she didn't." He went on, looking at Lyddy, "That as the time got nearer, she got more and more uptight at the thought of moving away. That you were unwilling to talk about it. That she felt she was burdening you to keep harping on about it." He paused. "That's about it, but she also said she didn't know how she was going to handle it, and that she didn't think she was going to handle it." He took Lyddy's hand in his, "Lyddy, she loves you so much, it stunned me."

Lyddy swallowed two mouthfuls, finishing her drink and let her glass rest in her lap. "Oh, Christ," she said quietly. "I've been so stupid." She held her glass out. Will picked the bottle up off the table and refilled her.

He grinned. "That's my girl."

Lyddy looked ruefully at the glass. "Yes, this will really help, won't it?" she said, the heavy sarcasm aimed at herself. "Get roaring drunk, that will really sort things out."

"Well," Will pushed her along, "now you've faced it. Before you lay yourself in a stupor," Lyddy managed a bleak smile at this, "are you going to think about how this can be resolved?"

"I don't need to think about it. It's been obvious all along. It's been pushed away to the back of my brain as well." She scoffed, "For the sake of expediency. God! I've been so stupid." She took a mouthful of her brandy.

"Well?" Will was relaxing now; Lyddy was in control. She could deal with it herself, but he wanted to be there to watch.

Lyddy thought of Chris's words. You only have one life. She looked at him and said simply, "We will have to move to Oxford."

Will couldn't help himself; he wanted to hear her answers, "What will you do with this house?"

"I'll sell it."

"What about your job?"

"I can get another job, can't I?"

"What about Peter in his new school?"

"He'll have to start another school up there. They have schools there, don't they?" she inquired of him.

The brandy was getting to her, he thought fondly, bringing back her sense of humour, albeit in sarcasm. "Annie will miss you," he said.

"Annie will have to come and visit, like all the rest, won't she? Anyway, she can bring the children down here to stay at holiday times. She won't have to look for excuses to have them, will she?"

Will was winding her up now, "What about me and Carl?"

"You and Carl will have to come and visit as well. And we can visit you. We all have cars, don't we?" Lyddy was beginning to slur her words.

"My darling Lyddy," said Will, "you never could take your drink, could you?"

"No, never." Lyddy took another swig.

"I seem to remember having to sit and watch you get drunk before."

"You do not have to sit there and watch me get drunk. You can go now. I am quite capable of getting drunk by myself."

"Well, before you pass out, one more question."

"What now?"

"Where will you live?"

Lyddy looked at him and smiled, a satisfied smile, "I know of a beautiful house for sale in Oxford."

"Live together?"

"Well, of course, live together." She expelled air through slightly parted lips in a rueful gesture. "If she'll have me."

Will didn't bother to respond to this. "Have you never thought of this before?" he asked.

Lyddy was silent for a moment as she considered this. "I've never faced it as an option." She stopped and closed her eyes briefly, "No, let's be honest, Lydia." She looked at Will. "I haven't let myself face it as an option. Christ! What an idiot." She tutted in exasperation at herself.

"You won't worry about what people will say? Neighbours? Colleagues?"

Lyddy looked at him askance. "That's rich, coming from you."

"Well? In the circumstances ..."

"I hardly need to answer that now, do I? With hindsight, I think anything that anyone might say pales to insignificance compared to the alternative." She had trouble getting her tongue around the words and laughed, "Well, love will out, or something like that." She grinned now, her truculence abating, all the questions answered to her satisfaction.

Will was content. "Oh, well. You've got it all sorted then. What the bloody hell am I doing here?"

"Will, my darling. What would I do without you?"

Will's expression remained deadpan. "Well, I can tell you one thing. No phoning me up from Oxford and sobbing into the phone. I'm damned if I'm racing up there, just to watch you get pissed."

Lyddy had to laugh. "Yes, that's a point. Can't you and Carl move too? I can't wait two hours for you to get there in an emergency."

Will took her hand, "What are you going to do now?"

"I'm going to get in the car and go and see Chris."

"Don't be so bloody stupid. You're way over the limit."

"I'm going to sleep this off and get in the car and go and see Chris."

"What? Today?"

"Yes. She looked at him, anticipation written all over her face, "I can't wait till tomorrow."

"Lyddy," he tutted at her, serious now, trying to reach her through the brandy. "Here you are, getting pleasantly drunk. You've solved it all in your head. Poor Chris is having a nervous breakdown; she's just been through the worst moment of her life. If she was a lesser individual, she'd be contemplating suicide now. At least phone her and put her out of her misery."

Lyddy thought for a moment. She pointedly put her drink to one side, discarded. "No," she said, "I can't rise to that." She grinned at Will, "I'll apologise to her in person."

"Oh, God! You have no heart."

"I do."

"Lyddy!" Will's tone gently scolded her.

"I'll make it up to her," Lyddy's grin was infectious now.

Will gave up. "Come on. Go to bed."

Lyddy started to push herself up off the sofa and fell back, giggling, "I can't get up."

"Oh, my God." Will pulled her to her feet and walked her upstairs, holding her elbow.

"How long do I need to sleep?" She stumbled on a step.

Will caught her and looked at his watch. "At least six hours."

"What!"

"Yes."

"Oh." She stopped at the top of the stairs as a thought struck her, "I need to phone Annie! The children!"

"I'll phone Annie. Where are they?"

She told him.

"Right. Don't give the children any more thought. It will be arranged."

"What? Will they stay at Annie's?"

"Yes, they will. And if they can't stay at Annie's, I'll come here and stay the night and baby-sit."

"Oh, Will! Carl's party!"

"He'll be the first to agree that this is more pressing."

"Oh, Will!"

"Don't worry about the children. Annie and I will sort them out."

He pulled the quilt aside on her bed, sat her down, pulled her shoes off and lifted her legs onto the bed.

She said, "Carl's present is on the dresser. It's not wrapped."

"Give it to him next time. Sleep! Ring me tomorrow."

"I will."

He drew the curtains across and bent to kiss her head.

"Will."

"What?"

"Thank you."

"You're welcome." He left the room.

Chapter Twenty

When Lyddy woke up, her head was thumping and it was dark. She looked at the clock to see how long she had slept. She swung her legs over the side of the bed and sat for a moment. She felt awful.

She put the landing light on and went into the bathroom to take two aspirins, then went to look in the children's room. Their beds were empty, their pyjamas and teddies gone. How did Annie manage that? she wondered. She had slept through it all. She went downstairs and switched the kitchen light on. Even Dodger was gone, and his bed. Everyone was seeing to her loose ends.

She made a cup of coffee and some toast and stood in the kitchen to have it, hoping her headache would go away. She remembered the scene with Will. Oh well, she probably deserved a bit of a headache. She thought of Chris; compared to what she must have been through all day, a headache was nothing. Lyddy felt guilty now, wishing she hadn't hit the bottle so hard. She didn't even like brandy.

She went upstairs and ran a bath while she undressed and threw a few things in a hold-all. After a quick bath she put on clean jeans, T-shirt and sweat shirt, grabbed a jacket and went downstairs. She locked up, switched the lights off and went outside to the car. Slipping a cassette into the car stereo, she pulled out of the drive.

When she arrived at Chris's it was nearly ten o'clock. Light was showing through the sitting room curtains and through the window above the front door. Lyddy felt nervous now and abject in her guilt. She'd had time during the drive to really think about how Chris must have felt, what she had put her through. Now, she was blithely turning up to tell her it was all sorted out and expecting her to say, "Jolly good, let's have a drink then."

She parked to the side of the house in front of the garage doors and got out, deciding to leave the hold-all in the car. Locking the car, she walked over to the front door and paused at the top of the steps. She rang the doorbell, feeling decidedly anxious. She waited a few moments, heard the click of the sitting room door and then the front door opened.

Chris opened the door wide as she saw Lyddy standing on the top step. Lyddy longed to step forward and put her arms round her, but she didn't. Chris was in a black T-shirt and jeans, bare feet, her hair wet, probably from the bath. She stared at Lyddy. With the light behind her, Lyddy couldn't see her face very clearly but her lovely features were set, her teeth clenched. She said nothing, just stared at Lyddy's face.

Lyddy didn't move. Her heart was breaking for Chris now, but she had no rights here. "Can I come in?" she asked quietly. Chris didn't respond at once. "Please," she urged.

Chris stepped aside without speaking. Lyddy passed through the front door and into the sitting room. It was warm in there, the fire banked up with coal, burning brightly. The room was lit by a lamp on the small table by the front window. A single violin played sadly, quietly, from the stereo.

Lyddy walked to the fire and gazed at the Naked Lady on the mantelpiece. She turned as Chris came into the room. She closed the door behind her and stood leaning her back against it, watching Lyddy, waiting for her to speak. She had that desolate look in her eyes. Lyddy realized with a start that Chris had lost a little weight. The slight hollow beneath her cheekbones was more pronounced. She bleakly wondered how she hadn't noticed before.

Lyddy stayed by the fire, looking at her, wondering where to start. "Chris," she took a breath and said with feeling, "I'm so sorry. What I've done to you is unforgivable." She paused to think. "Now, with hindsight, I don't know how I could have let you become so miserable. I don't know how I could have let things come to this. I knew how you felt. God knows you tried to tell me enough times and," she stopped in disbelief at herself, "I just fobbed you off or made light of it or told you it would get better, or side-stepped it." She looked at Chris now, shaking her head a little, "I'm so sorry. I've been incredibly stupid. I love you so much, the thought of being without you," she searched for the word, "it's unbearable. I can't even contemplate it."

Chris pushed herself away from the door and opened her mouth to speak.

Lyddy put her hand up, "Let me finish. I have to do this." She thought for a moment. "I have to be honest and say that the thought of ever being without you has only occurred to me today, for the first time, and I find it devastating. I hadn't even considered before this, that you might one day not be there. I have blithely let you go on getting more and more miserable and I took it all for granted that you would cope and we would just go on."

Lyddy put her hand on her chest in her incredulity at herself as she now put all this into words. "You say that I'm the strong one, that I can cope because I can push things out of my mind." She looked up again, "That's not strength, is it? Putting your head in the sand. Dealing with problems by ignoring them. You're the strong one. You have wanted to face this all along and I talked you out of it," she frowned, "or I didn't talk to you about it at all." She paused while she reflected. "What you did this morning took more courage than I could ever find. It must have been so hard for you."

In her agitation, Lyddy turned round to look at the fire, considering her behaviour and finding it bewildering now. She turned back towards Chris, "How can you love me? I have been so selfish." She didn't wait for an answer. "And on top of all that, I have been totally supported by my family, my friends. Not a single one of them has made this hard for me. Whereas," she thought back, "you have had to cope with your parents, their hurt and their outrage. Of your friends, only Maggie has been really supportive. Most of the rest, well..." she stopped. "It must have been so difficult for you. And I've just let you bear it all. How can you have loved me so much?" She looked now to Chris in honest wonder. She had never faced up to her failings before, hadn't even realised them.

Chris's expression had changed to concern. She came over and held Lyddy's face in her hands, gazing at her. "You're being too hard on yourself," she said quietly. "It's not your fault. You can't be responsible for my parents."

"No," said Lyddy, softly, hating herself at this moment, "but I could have helped you."

Chris went on, "You put a brave face on things. That's not a fault. You did what you thought was best."

"I didn't. I did what I thought was easiest."

"Oh, Lyddy. You can't blame yourself for all this."

"I can. If I lose you I can blame myself." Lyddy looked into Chris's face, tears threatening, "Chris, I can't lose you, I couldn't bear it."

Chris put her arms out and Lyddy fell into them. She held on to Chris and said again, "I couldn't bear it." They stood for a while, hugging each other in front of the fire.

Lyddy drew her head back so that she could look at Chris. She was more controlled now. "I'm so sorry. That I allowed you to get to the state you were in this morning is unforgivable. I want to be with you, come home to you, love you, live with you."

Chris gave her a small smile, "You can't know how glad I am to hear you say that. This has been the worst day of my life."

"Oh, Chris."

They kissed and Lyddy pushed her tongue almost aggressively into Chris's mouth, a desperate passion in her, that she might have lost her and never held her again, that she had driven her to do what she did.

When they drew apart, Lyddy was calmer. She looked at Chris, "Will you forgive me?"

Chris smiled gently at her, "I never blamed you. There's nothing to forgive."

"Will you have me back?"

Chris's eyes moved over Lyddy's face. "Lyddy, I've never wanted anything more in the whole world." A slight frown creased her forehead, "I can't live like we were, I would go insane. I can't live half with you and half without you."

Lyddy looked at her, "How much is Mrs Everton asking for this house?"

Chris was slightly taken aback. She told her the figure.

Lyddy did a quick calculation in her head. "How do you fancy buying it?"

"I couldn't afford it."

"No, with me. Buying it with me, going halves, or something?"

Chris wasn't quite with her. "You would own two houses?"

"No, I'll sell mine." Lyddy's look expressed her genuine amazement at their stupidity. She said, "It should have been so obvious."

It was starting to dawn on Chris, but she was still a few steps behind Lyddy. "What about your job?"

"I'll look for another one."

Chris was smiling now. "What about the children's schools?"

Lyddy was recovering her equilibrium, "Oh, bloody hell," she said. "I've had to go through all this today with Will. The children can change schools, can't they?" She went on before Chris could speak again, "And now you're going to ask me, 'What about Annie? What about Will? What about Great-Aunt-Fanny?' They can bloody come and visit us, can't they, if they want to see us? And no, I don't give a toss what people might say. For God's sake!" Her relief was coming out in her belligerence. "Am I the only one with any sense? Do I have to spell it out to everyone?"

Chris laughed and hugged her, "Would you really?"

"Really what?"

"Don't be obtuse. Would you really sell your house, change your job, put the children in new schools to come up here to live?"

Lyddy was herself again. "Of course I bloody would!"

Chris laughed again, "Stop swearing. It's not becoming." Her look changed, something had dawned. "What do you mean – you had to go through all this with Will today?"

Lyddy looked guilty. She had been caught out.

"When did you decide you were coming to live up here?"

Lyddy was sheepish now. "About one o'clock. I'm not sure exactly. I was a bit drunk. Will filled me with brandy."

Chris was incredulous, "Ha! Will filled you with brandy! What did he do? Hold your nose and pour it down your throat?" She looked at the clock, "You mean you decided this nearly ten hours ago and you're only just telling me now? Was the phone out of order? What have you been doing since then?"

"Sleeping."

"Sleeping!"

"Oh, God. Don't talk to Will about this, will you?"

Chris couldn't hide her amusement at Lyddy's discomfort. "Why?"

"Because he told me I should ring you."

"What did you say?"

"I said you would have to wait to hear it in person, or words to that effect," she finished lamely.

"Lyddy! How could you? All those hours of near-suicidal misery! You could have picked up the phone and said, 'Chris, I'll sell the house. We'll move to Oxford'."

"No, I couldn't. I had to see you," Lyddy was adamant. Her face broke into a devilish grin, "I did tell Will I would make it up to you."

"Did you?"

"Yes."

"Will you?"

"Yes."

A smile spread over Chris's face as she considered this information, the misery and frustration of the last few weeks forgotten. "What, now? Here in front of the fire?"

"Yes."

They both grinned and wrapped their arms round each other. Chris looked at Lyddy, her happiness evident in her shining eyes, "Well?"

Lyddy took the cue, "Oh! Well, I have to undress you first."

"Oh, good."

They didn't speak as she first undressed Chris in front of the fire, tossing her clothes in a heap on a chair, then took her own off to join them. They stood naked facing each other, Chris waiting, forcing Lyddy to make the move. She looked gorgeous; Lyddy couldn't contain herself. She slipped her arms around Chris, fitting her bare body to hers. Then she kissed her, opening her mouth wide, sliding her hands all over her body, moving her hips against hers. They moaned with the sheer pleasure of it. Then Lyddy brought them both gently to the carpet, the warmth of the fire on their bodies. She lay Chris on her back and reached across to a chair to take a cushion to put under her head. She sat on the floor, up close, with her legs to one side and leaned on one hand, looking down at her.

Chris slipped her arm up around Lyddy's bare back and rubbed her hand over it. She glanced at the fire and back, smiling up at Lyddy. "This is where we started out, isn't it?" she said quietly.

Lyddy ran her hand gently over Chris's body, her eyes roaming over it in the firelight. "Yes," she said, distractedly, "more or less."

"Lyddy."

"Hm?"

"I'm so glad you're here. You can't imagine."

"Oh, yes I can." Lyddy's eyes followed her hand as she moved it very slowly over Chris's breasts, down across her tummy, over her hips and then ran it along her upper leg. She brought her hand back again, running it up as far as it would go between Chris's legs. Chris parted them slightly, pushing the small of her back to the floor. Lyddy looked at her, into her brown eyes, her own expression intent, serious. "To think I might have lost you," she murmured, her hand still moving.

Chris spread her knees wide, closing her eyes. "Lyddy," her voice came out as a breathy whisper, "stop babbling."

"Yes, my darling. With pleasure." She had to make it up to her. She moved to lay between Chris's legs and let her mouth follow the same passage again with her hands, but this time infinitely more slowly. Chris let out a low moan and took Lyddy's head in her hands. Lyddy lifted her mouth for a second with a grin, "I hope you're not in a hurry, this is going to take some time."

Chris groaned and lifted her hips to move them against Lyddy's body and uttered in the same breathy voice, "Lyddy... shut up!"

They made some sandwiches, opened some wine, put some more music on and sat into the night by the fire, making their plans, doing their sums, working out the logistics of it all.

Lyddy decided she would put the house on the market straight away. Chris had some savings to put into the new house and would take out a mortgage, but Lyddy would need to sell her house before they could buy.

They talked about how long it might take her to find a new job within a reasonable travelling distance. It was now mid-October, only two months to the end of term. They couldn't count on there being a suitable job vacancy and her getting it in that time. Lyddy decided to give in her notice as soon as she got back to school after half-term. The sale of the house she had shared with David had left a reasonable lump sum after buying her present one, and she hadn't had reason to delve into it much. If necessary, she could live off that until she found work.

"It will use up your nest-egg," Chris said. They were sitting on the sofa, legs sprawled in front of them, the plate of sandwiches finished.

"I could probably live for about three years on it if I had to. I won't have a mortgage."

"Are you sure about this?" Chris asked her.

Lyddy put her hand on Chris's leg and looked at her affectionately, "Of course I am. That means we'll be living together by Christmas, only about eight weeks away."

Chris put her head back and heaved a sigh, "What a wonderful thought."

"Well, there you are, then. It's worth the children and me living on bread and jam and wearing rags for a while, isn't it?"

"You just said you could live for about three years without a job," Chris accused her.

"I'm just being histrionic."

"Well, don't. Be serious for once. Anyway, you can get on the supply register to earn some money. Next question. What about your house? You won't sell it and complete by Christmas, will you?"

Lyddy thought for a moment. She said, "Do you think Mrs Everton would let us rent until we can buy it from her? Take the house off the market, I mean?"

"She might. I'll phone her tomorrow. She's a very nice woman. She didn't seem to be in a great hurry. I don't think she needs the money urgently."

"Right. That's that. What else?"

They both thought for a moment, if they had missed anything.

Lyddy said, "The bed. That enormous bed."

"What about it?"

"Ask her if we can buy it from her."

"Good Lord, Lyddy. You accuse me of having a one-track mind. You're totally reorganising your whole life and you are worrying about a bed."

"I'm being practical," Lyddy answered lightly. "Ask her."

Chris put her head on Lyddy's shoulder, "I can hardly believe all this."

A thought struck Lyddy. She looked at Chris, their faces up close, "Did you ever think of this? That I could move up here?"

"Of course I did."

"Oh, my God. Why didn't you say something?"

"Lyddy, I couldn't have asked you to sell your house, leave your job, move the children. For me."

Lyddy was exasperated at her, "Oh, how stupid!"

"Don't call me stupid."

"Oh, Chris. I wish you had said something."

Chris took her hand and said, "What would you have said? 'Oh, yes, why didn't I think of that? I'll put the house on the market tomorrow. I'll give in my notice too'." She stopped and Lyddy just looked at her. Chris said gently, "Staying at each other's houses is one thing; actually living together is something else. The repercussions of it all; laying yourself open." She squeezed Lyddy's hand to help soften the blow, "You wouldn't have, would you? Not twenty-four hours ago."

Lyddy gazed at Chris and then rested her head on the back of the sofa. She emitted a long sigh. "No, you're probably right." She twisted her neck to glance at Chris, "It's me that's been stupid." They were both silent for a moment and then Lyddy said, "You could have tried me. You could have talked to me, made me talk about it."

"No, I couldn't. It doesn't matter now, does it?"

"I've been a real coward, haven't I? We could have been saved all that misery and aggro." She closed her eyes, feeling quite dejected at her lack of moral courage.

"It doesn't matter now. Don't start again! Anyway, it was worth it, to see you beating your breast at the fireplace." Chris tried to keep a straight face, but failed.

"What!" Lyddy's eyes shot open to look at her.

"I had to stop myself laughing at one point."

"You didn't! When was that?"

"When you said," Chris put on a theatrical tone of self-chastisement, "How can you love me? I have been so selfish!" She threw out her arms as she spoke. "Very melodramatic. I think you thought you were back in school. Self-abasement with 3C."

Lyddy was indignant, "You're laughing at me! I come up here, throw myself on your mercy, thoroughly berate my own character, selflessly admit all my faults for open scrutiny. And you're laughing at me!"

"Yes, alright. Don't lay it on. Two can play at your game,"

"What game?"

"Taking the piss all the time."

"I do not take the piss all the time!"

"Oh, here we go." Chris was emphatic, "Yes, you do."

Lyddy finished her wine and stood up. "Well, I'm going to bed. I'm not staying here to be laughed at."

"I'll come with you. I can laugh at you upstairs."

"You're intolerable when you're happy." Lyddy stood at the door, waiting while Chris put the guard in front of the fire and switched off the stereo and the light. Still trying to recoup some dignity, she added, "You'd better watch yourself if you're expecting to come and stay at my house for the rest of this holiday."

Chris walked over to join her at the doorway. "You'd better watch yourself if you're expecting to sleep in *my* bed for the rest of tonight." They linked arms as they went through the house to the stairs.

Chapter Twenty-One

On the day that Lyddy and the children finally moved into the big house with Chris, they held a small ceremony at the front door whereby they all had to step over the threshold at the same moment in time. Their move was heralded by all four of them getting stuck in the doorway and landing in a tangled heap in the hall, amidst silly giggles and shrieks.

The end of the autumn term had been a busy time for Lyddy, putting on a play with the lower school, as well as Christmas shopping to be done. She had felt she couldn't get organized enough to move before Christmas. So they spent Christmas and New Year at Lyddy's and moved the day after, giving them a few days before Chris started back to work and the children started their new schools. Mrs Everton had arranged to have her furniture removed during the holiday except for the items which Chris and Lyddy had bought from her. Lyddy moved everything into the new house, leaving the old one empty. They spent the day deciding where it should all go and moving Chris's belongings out of the second bedroom to distribute around the house. Peter asked if he could have a bedroom to himself now that he was eight and after some arguments they decided that he would have the larger one at the front and Nikki the back bedroom.

Nikki and Peter had taken the news of the move with the excited enthusiasm of children, once they had been assured that their rabbits would be going with them. Nikki declared they would have to play hide and seek every day. Their grandad was sworn to come and stay, when the weather was warmer, to help them build the tree house. He was delighted at the move. They were now within twenty minutes drive of him. Lyddy and Chris resigned themselves to having to humour him more often, putting up with his facetious remarks at their expense.

Annie had received the news of the impending move with remarkable alacrity, Lyddy thought. In fact, when Lyddy told her, she said, "Well, I'm surprised you didn't think of it before. Really, for an intelligent woman, Lyddy, you are sometimes very slow off the mark." She made anxious inquiries, of course, as to whether the children would be able to come and stay with her during the holidays.

After they had decided on the move, Chris phoned her parents to tell them that she and Lyddy were going to live together, buy a house together. Her mother simply said, "Oh, Chris." Chris suggested that it was time they met Lyddy, and she replied again, "No, I can't. I'm sorry. I just can't." When her father came on the phone, Chris thought he sounded more amenable than in the past, asking questions about Lyddy's job, the children, when Lyddy would move. Questions which broached the subject in a way he hadn't before. He said quietly, though, "I hope you're doing the right thing, love." Chris went to see them on Boxing Day on her own, staying one night with them. Her mother continued to evade the subject of Lyddy during their conversations but her father was more open when Chris was alone with him.

The sale of Lyddy's house and the purchase of the new one went ahead in February. Mrs Everton had been pleased to find a buyer so easily, and was happy that someone she knew was to have the home that she and her husband had shared for thirty years.

Lyddy hadn't found a job by the time they moved. She had the disadvantage that she had only been back in teaching for a relatively short time and before that had had a few years' break. She wasn't worried. She gave herself a couple of weeks off after Christmas to get things done and to see the children settled into their new schools. Then she applied to go on the Register of Supply Teachers, covering absences for the area. She got some work with two of the local secondary schools and just before half term she was offered almost a term's work, covering maternity leave up to the half term holiday at the beginning of June, which she accepted.

During the time she was off work, Lyddy got to know one of their neighbours, Linda, who lived across the road a few doors up. Linda's younger son was at the same school as Nikki and her other one went to school with Peter. Lyddy invited Linda and her husband over for dinner one Saturday, which they accepted and in due course returned the invitation. Lyddy and Chris didn't know if Linda and John were aware of their relationship. Chris said they must be daft if they hadn't realised, and Lyddy said it didn't matter anyway. When Lyddy first started getting work, a day here, two days there, Linda offered to take the children to school for her and to meet them in the afternoon. When she accepted full-time work they made it a semi-permanent arrangement. It was a God-send for Lyddy. Chris couldn't help her out now as she was always gone by seven thirty in the morning and was seldom home before six. They eased into a routine whereby Lyddy cooked for them all during the week and Chris took over at weekends.

Mrs Everton's cleaner gave in her notice after Lyddy had moved in, when she became aware of the sleeping arrangements. They managed to find another, Mrs Larks. She became known affectionately in the household as 'Call Me Madge'. She was wonderful, busy, cheerful. On the days Lyddy was there, Madge would bustle out of the room half-way through a conversation and come back in half an hour later to continue it as though she hadn't been away. Her understanding of the extent of Lyddy and Chris's relationship had been immediate. Without making too much of a public announcement of it, Lyddy had deliberately shown her round the house before she accepted the job, to give her the opportunity to decline at the outset, saving possible embarrassment later. It became a favourite topic in Madge's ceaseless chatter, "Of course, you never know what goes on, do you, behind closed doors? Live and let live, I say. If it doesn't hurt me, then I can't complain, can I?" She would deliver one of her cheerful beams, "As long as folks are happy, that's what counts," and would bustle out again, armed with clean duster. When Lyddy was working, she would come home on a Friday to find an apple pie in the fridge or a pot of home-made soup and a note, "Save you some time tonight, dear. Madge."

Dodger was a problem on work days, until Lyddy got talking one day to an elderly couple who lived five doors down. They stopped to talk to Dodger, telling Lyddy all about their dog who had died the year before. Mr Samuel wouldn't let his wife have another, she had been so heart-broken on the death of theirs. He couldn't go through that again. When Lyddy met them on a further occasion, they had offered to help out with Dodger when she was working. They ended up taking him home with them for part of the day, as Mr Burberry had done, thoroughly spoiling him there.

Everything was working out, Lyddy thought contentedly.

Chris's parents remained a blot on their landscape but Chris thought her mum would come round eventually. Her dad was apparently doing his best with her.

Lyddy was sitting at the kitchen table with the Times Educational Supplement spread out in front of her, looking through the job vacancies. It was the first week of the Easter holidays, Thursday. The children were over at Linda's for the morning. Linda's son Jack, who had just had his ninth birthday, had a new go-kart. Lyddy was working herself up to giving the lawn its first cut of the year, but sat on by her empty coffee cup, browsing through the ads. They were having a belated house-warming party on Saturday, in the garden. The weather forecast was good. Chris had gone to do a big food shop to get them through the weekend and to stock up with drink for the party. She had insisted that they never go food shopping together. She said it was the mark of a stale relationship and that things could only go downhill after trudging round the supermarket discussing whether they needed toilet rolls. She also knew how much Lyddy hated supermarket shopping.

Lyddy glanced at her watch. Chris would be back soon and she hadn't even got the lawn mower out yet. She started as she heard the front door open and jumped up. She went through the hall to take some bags from Chris.

"Hello, my darling," Chris leaned forward to touch her lips to Lyddy's. "Cut the grass, yet?" Her look told Lyddy that she knew the answer perfectly well.

Lyddy grinned guiltily, "I've found a job to apply for."

Chris laughed as she carried bags of shopping to the kitchen, "What you mean is, you've been sitting on your bum reading the paper."

"No, I haven't. Yes, I have," Lyddy decided to be honest.

She followed her with more bags and dumped them on the table. "But I have found a job. It would suit me down to the ground." She pointed out the advert to Chris who read it through. It was for a drama specialist in an independent school.

"Four to twelve year olds," Chris read. "That would be different."

"Well, I think I should get out of secondary," Lyddy said. The environment had never really suited her. It was all too stuffy for her liking. Less marking too, she thought.

Chris finished reading it. "It would be perfect for you." She glanced at the advert again, "To start in September." She pecked Lyddy on the cheek before she went back to get the rest of the shopping, raising her voice to be heard as she walked out of the kitchen, "Go for it, you'll probably get it. I don't want to end up supporting you lot. You eat too much."

Lyddy circled the advert with a felt-tip pen and folded the paper. She started putting the shopping away in cupboards.

Chris came back in. "I've just seen the chap who lives over the road."

"What, the one who drives out with a different girl each morning?"

"Yes, his name's Alan. He tried to chat me up going round Sainsbury's."

"Did he really?"

"He asked me out on Saturday."

"Did he? What did you say?"

"I said we were having a party on Saturday. Would he like to come. I said he could meet my girlfriend."

Lyddy laughed. "What did he say?"

"He looked rather crestfallen and asked if he could bring someone. So I said yes, and that I expected one of his girlfriends would be available. He laughed."

Lyddy said, "Oh, good. We *are* getting to know the neighbours."

Chris switched the kettle on and came over to put her arms round Lyddy, smiling, "Yes, except we can't invite them all to a party in a field. Are you going to cut the grass?"

"You're a hard woman."

"I've just pushed a shopping trolley round for an hour so now you can go and push the mower round for an hour. I'll put the rest of this away," she nodded towards the shopping.

"Can I have a coffee first?"

"No, I'll bring one out to you. Stop procrastinating." She kissed Lyddy on the lips.

"Oh, a woman's work..." Lyddy started towards the back door.

"Yes, quite," said Chris. "I'll get lunch when you've finished that. Your children will be back soon, starving hungry."

Chapter Twenty-Two

"Good God! Where did you get sheets big enough for that?" Will exclaimed as Lyddy showed him into the main bedroom.

Lyddy smiled as she took his arm, "The previous owner left them, and a duvet. We bought the bed from her with the house."

"That's not a bed. That's a free-fall parachute landing stage for beginners." He laughed, "If you two fall out, you won't have to sleep on the sofa. You can tell her you're sleeping on the other side tonight."

They walked over to the window seat and sat down, drinks in hand. Lyddy had been showing Will round the house. It was the first time he and Carl had been up to see them. They had cancelled a previously arranged visit because they both had flu.

"Well, what do you think?" Lyddy asked.

"Of the bed?"

"No! Of the house!"

"It's lovely." He glanced at her, their arms still linked, "Very you. Old, but maintaining its charm."

"Thank you, my darling. Compliments like that I can do without."

Will looked at her now. He hadn't seen her since Christmas. "You were blooming with life before, my love. Now you are radiant. Do you always look so disgustingly happy these days?"

"Well, if you came to see us more often..."

"We will. It's just been a busy couple of months." He smiled at her, "Things are going well, I take it?"

Lyddy took a sip of her wine and said without hesitation, "Will, I've never been so happy in my life."

"I can see that." He smiled. "Well, who would have thought it?"

"Who indeed!"

"Chris is obviously just as content as you. She's radiating a state of euphoric bliss as well. What are you two doing to each other?"

"Mind your own business."

"Mind you, with a bed that size..."

Lyddy laughed. She didn't let him finish. "You're as bad as she is." She turned her face to him, "It's lovely to see you. I've missed you."

"Carl suggested on the way up here that we should all have a week off somewhere. In the summer." He added, "He likes Chris."

"Because she laughs at his awful jokes." Lyddy thought about his suggestion. "That would be fun. Annie might have the children. She misses them. She's been on about taking them to Eurodisney for a few days. They'll be pleased; two holidays in France. We're all going to Brittany for a fortnight as well."

"Right. We'll arrange a date," Will said. He glanced at her, "How are your feminist principles standing up to events?"

"Very well, thank you."

"Not shaken a little at the foundations?"

"Not at all."

"Not worried that you'll be hung under the umbrella of false misconceptions?"

"No. I don't care what they hang me under."

"Ah! I sense a subtle change of tack!"

She grinned, "I just don't care. But nothing's changed; I am who I am; I'm still my own boss." She stopped. "Oh no! I'm not getting drawn into that again."

Will laughed, "Refusing the bait?"

"Yes, I am." She gave him a determined look, "You'll have to look elsewhere to satisfy your waggish sense of humour."

"What a pity." He pulled her up with him by her arm, "You'd better get back to your party, then." They walked out of the room to go downstairs. "How are the neighbours? Open-minded?"

Lyddy caught the significance of his question, remembering the tales Carl had told of their neighbours at the flat. "They're fine. We didn't put a notice up when we moved in, mind you. There's been no problem. We lost the first cleaning lady, though," she smiled.

Will raised his eyebrows and looked towards the ceiling. "One of the potential pit-falls," he said. As they got to the bottom of the stairs, he leant over to kiss her cheek, "I'm absolutely delighted for you. At least I won't be getting any more of those bloody phone calls."

Lyddy pecked him on the cheek in response and started to follow him into the kitchen. The doorbell rang urgently and she turned to walk down the hall. When she opened the door Rose stepped in, flung her arms wide and wrapped them around Lyddy. "We made it! We got lost again. All these damned roads look the same." She smacked a kiss on Lyddy's cheek. "You look wonderful."

"Hello, Rose." Lyddy returned her hug and turned to Tweedie coming in behind, "Tweedie, let me take that." She took the holdall from her and put it inside the sitting room doorway. Rose and Tweedie were staying the night. "I'm glad you could come."

"Hello, Lyddy." Tweedie clutched Lyddy's hand briefly and nodded towards Rose, "We'll have to watch her. She's planning to hit the bottle."

"Good, that should keep us all amused." Lyddy grinned at Rose's happy face and looked back to Tweedie, "It's lovely to see you again."

"Where's the booze?" Rose demanded. "I'm parched."

Lyddy walked with them towards the kitchen. "Don't get too drunk, Rose. You have to behave yourself until the neighbours have gone."

"I'll be the model of decorum."

"I find that hard to imagine."

"Don't worry! I'm good with neighbours."

Something in her tone made Tweedie laugh, "Rose!" She said to Lyddy, "I'll stick to her like a limpet till they've all gone."

Rose put her arm round Tweedie's waist and nibbled her ear, "Mm, I'm going to enjoy this."

Lyddy laughed as she led the way into the kitchen. She poured them both a drink and Will came over to say hello. They had all met at Christmas at Lyddy's. Lyddy told them she was going to check everyone was alright and left them with Will. She moved across the kitchen towards Carl who was talking to two of Chris's friends. They were laughing uproariously at something he had said. Lyddy was pleased. They had been taken aback, to say the least, when they first met Lyddy the previous June. It had been a little awkward and the friendship had subsequently cooled somewhat. Chris had been a bit upset, but she decided that they should invite them to the party.

"They can come or they can make an excuse and not come." They had phoned to say that they would love to come. One out of three, not bad, Lyddy thought. The other two had made excuses.

Grabbing a bottle from the table as she passed, she went over to them, "Can I top anyone up?"

Anne held out her glass, "Please. I'm alright today. Simon's driving. We tossed for it." She smiled back at Lyddy, "I love the house, Lyddy. Chris showed me round when we got here."

"Thank you. So do we."

Carl and Simon stood to one side, continuing their conversation with bursts of laughter every now and then.

Anne said, "I'm glad you invited us. I've mentally kicked myself a few times. I thought Chris and I were going to lose touch." Her expression was a little rueful, "I didn't know how to break the ice."

Lyddy liked her frank honesty. She said, "Chris was really pleased when you said you could come."

Anne turned her back slightly on the men and lowered her voice, "Are Will and Carl... gay?"

Lyddy grinned. "Yes, they are."

"I just wondered. I like them; Carl's had us in fits here. Have you known them long?"

"Will's my oldest friend," Lyddy told her. "You know the sort of thing, always there in an emergency."

"You're lucky. Chris was probably the closest I've ever got to that." She reflected for a moment and put her hand affectionately on Lyddy's arm, "I'm so glad we came today."

Lyddy understood why she and Chris were friends. She briefly pressed Anne's hand with hers. "So am I. You'll have to come and stay one weekend. Peter can move in with Nikki for the night. Meanwhile," she put her glass down and picked up another opened bottle from the kitchen worktop, "I'd better circulate the booze. I'll see you later."

Anne smiled at her in reply and turned back to the men.

Lyddy stepped outside into the garden. The weather had fulfilled the forecast. It was gloriously sunny, showing off the garden. Jane came up behind her and slipped her arm through Lyddy's, holding out her empty glass. They stood still while Lyddy topped her up.

"Where have you been?" Lyddy asked.

"In the loo." She grinned at Lyddy, something obviously on her mind.

"What?" Lyddy had to smile at her expectant expression.

"Um... Does the lovely Maggie have a husband?"

"Jane!" Lyddy laughed. "It's not a prerequisite of coming to see us, you know."

Jane's grin broadened, "Does she?"

"Yes, she does, a newish one. He's in Manchester today, a conference or something."

"Oh, shucks," she giggled.

"How many bottles have you had?"

"This is only my second glass, actually." She sipped her drink and changed the subject, "I've decided you have to make things happen."

"Yes, so I gather."

"No, I don't mean that." She looked at Lyddy with smiling eyes, "I've applied to Bristol University. To do a degree in Women's Studies."

"Good Lord! Good for you."

"Yes, that's what I thought." She laughed shortly, "I won't tell you what Jack thinks."

"Bristol?"

"Yes, it's going to take some arranging. Kids and everything. I can do part-time, four years."

Lyddy was impressed. "What brought this on?"

Jane considered this as she looked around the garden, "I don't know really... Life slipping by... Lack of purpose." She focused on Lyddy's face, "Bringing up the kids, it's not enough. I need to get involved."

Lyddy waited; she obviously had more to add. The sound of laughter burst from the kitchen.

Jane hesitated to say what was on her mind. Then she said, "It was you and Chris, your derring-do." She smiled self-consciously, out of character, "It just inspired me somehow."

Lyddy squeezed her arm affectionately, "How gratifying. I think it's a brilliant idea."

"Yes. I think life's about to change." She was silent for a moment, contemplating this, then she stirred herself, "Right, back to the party." She laid her hand briefly on Lyddy's shoulder in parting.

Lyddy watched her walking down the garden, feeling curiously delighted. Then she saw Chris coming towards her and walked to meet her. She was clearly enjoying herself.

"Hello, my love," Lyddy said. "Rose and Tweedie have arrived."

Chris came up close to Lyddy and kept her voice low, although no one was within earshot, "Shall we get rid of all these people and go upstairs?"

A contented smile spread over Lyddy's face. She kept her voice low as well, "Tempting. You've been at the booze."

"I know. What do you say?"

Lyddy held up the bottles she was about to take round. "I say good job one of us is showing some sense of responsibility and good manners."

Chris laughed at her, unabashed.

Lyddy went on, "Go and see Anne. I've just been talking to her. She's being entertained by Carl. Rose is in there too, in fighting form. You'd better go and rescue Anne before she's corrupted any more than necessary." She looked happily into Chris's face, adding, "And don't drink too much or you'll pass out. I won't be able to take advantage of you when everyone's gone."

"I won't pass out. I would never waste such an opportunity." Chris glanced at the bottles in Lyddy's hands, "I fancy the waitress too much."

She carried on towards the kitchen and Lyddy looked round as she walked down the garden; everyone was scattered in small groups. All the children were playing around the apple tree. They had put up a rope ladder to one branch and Lyddy's father had tied an old tyre to another. She saw her father was talking to Mr and Mrs Samuel, the dog-walking neighbours. They were sitting at the picnic table; Dodger sprawled under the table across Mrs Samuel's feet. Jane had rejoined Maggie's group; Jack was there and Linda and her husband, their neighbours from down the road. Annie's husband, Bob, was standing with Alan, from across the road. He and Bob were in the same line of business. Alan had a brunette hanging on his arm. Annie was engrossed in conversation with Muriel, one of the teachers at Chris's school. They made an odd couple. Muriel was something of a Bohemian, in her fifties, very individual in both her dress and her attitudes to life – very brash and open. Chris said she was super with the kids at school. Lyddy liked her. She smiled to herself, wondering what Annie would have to say later.

Annie and Muriel were the closest to the house so Lyddy made towards them. Nikki came running over before she got to them.

"Mum!"

"Hello, sweetheart. Are you having a good time?"

"Yes, lovely! Mum, can we have the paddling pool out?"

"No, it's not warm enough."

"But it's sunny! And we're all baking."

"Nikki, no. We discussed this earlier."

"Well, I'm disgusting it again."

Lyddy laughed, "Discussing. It's discussing."

"Well, I'm discussing it again!"

"No, we're not. You're not having it out. You'd all be freezing cold in five minutes"

"Oh, Mum."

Lyddy bent to kiss the top of her head, "While you're up here, go into the kitchen. Chris will find you another bottle of lemonade to take down with you."

Nikki was diverted, "When are we going to eat? I'm starving."

"In a little while. Go and get the lemonade," she raised her voice as Nikki ran off towards the kitchen, "and say please."

"Ye-es, Mu-um!"

Lyddy continued her way towards Annie and Muriel, holding out the bottles in her hand.

Annie turned towards her, "Oh, Lyddy. Yes please." Annie held out her glass. She seemed quite animated. "Muriel's been telling me about her life. It's fascinating."

Muriel directed a wide beam at Lyddy, "We've got as far as the rice boat down the Yangtze."

Lyddy smiled as she topped up their glasses. She had heard these stories. Muriel had taken five years off in her thirties, spent all her savings on travels around Asia, working her way where she could.

Annie continued, "All those places! All those adventures! I must say it makes our holidays abroad seem very banal by comparison."

She turned back to Muriel, quite enthralled, "So where did you sleep? I mean, in an open boat, with a Chinese family all aboard?"

Lyddy managed to stop her bottom jaw from dropping. Annie was tipsy. Lyddy had never before seen Annie drink more than she could comfortably handle. She never allowed herself to drop her guard, in or out of company. Lyddy was amazed. She stood watching Annie with fond amusement, as Muriel continued with her story.

Nikki came running by, clutching a bottle of lemonade and a large variety pack of crisps. "Someone else's come, Mum," she called as she skipped past.

Lyddy turned to look towards the house. A couple in their late fifties were coming round the side of the house. They had come up the path alongside the garage. Lyddy hadn't seen them before. They stood a little uncertainly at the corner of the house, searching the groups of people standing around in the garden.

Lyddy's heart lurched. She passed one bottle to Annie and one to Muriel to take in their free hands, muttered, "Excuse me," and started walking towards the couple, her heart somewhere up in her throat. The man was tall, greying at the temples; the woman had an attractive face for her years, her features slightly pinched at this moment, betraying some nervousness.

They looked at Lyddy as she approached. She smiled at them, her expression belying the turmoil in her, "Hello!" She maintained her smile of greeting as she allowed them to introduce themselves.

The man stepped forward, "Lyddy?"

"Yes."

He returned Lyddy's smile and put out his hand, "I'm John Carter, Chris's father."

Lyddy took his hand firmly and looked into his face. "Yes," she said, "I thought you must be. I'm very pleased to meet you."

John Carter took his wife's arm and said, "This is Eve, Chris's mother."

Lyddy smiled again and held out her hand. "Thank you for coming," she said. "Chris will be over the moon."

Eve Carter took her hand, lightly, but she held it for a few moments as she spoke, "I'm glad to meet you." Lyddy thought she was going to say 'at last'. Eve looked a little abashed and added, "I didn't know what to expect."

What had she thought? Big biceps, rough work-worn hands and corduroy trousers? It didn't matter. She said, "Chris is in the kitchen." She started walking with them and said again, "She'll be so pleased."

As they got to the back door, she heard Rose's voice and then a roar of laughter. It died down and Lyddy leant in to call across the kitchen, "Chris!"